Anton *and* Cecil
Cats Aloft

Also by Lisa Martin and Valerie Martin
Anton and Cecil: Cats at Sea
Anton and Cecil: Cats on Track

Anton *and* Cecil
Cats Aloft

By LISA MARTIN *and*
VALERIE MARTIN

Illustrated by KELLY MURPHY

ALGONQUIN YOUNG READERS   2016

Published by
Algonquin Young Readers
an imprint of Algonquin Books of Chapel Hill
P.O. Box 2225
Chapel Hill, NC 27515-2225

a division of
Workman Publishing
225 Varick Street
New York, New York 10014

LIBRARY OF CONGRESS CATALOGING-IN-PUBLICATION DATA
Names: Martin, Lisa, [date] author. | Martin, Valerie, [date] author.
Title: Anton and Cecil : cats aloft / Lisa Martin and Valerie Martin.
Other titles: Cats aloft
Description: First edition. | Chapel Hill, North Carolina : Algonquin
Young Readers, 2016. | Summary: "Cat brothers Anton and Cecil team up
with a police dog to search for missing puppies at the Chicago World's Fair
in the thrilling final installment to the series"—Provided by publisher.
Identifiers: LCCN 2016018799 | ISBN 9781616204594
Subjects: LCSH: World's Columbian Exposition (1893: Chicago, Ill.)—
Juvenile fiction. | Cats—Juvenile fiction. | Brothers—Juvenile fiction. | Quests
(Expeditions)—Juvenile fiction. | Animals—Juvenile fiction. | Adventure
stories. | CYAC: Cats—Fiction. | Brothers—Fiction. | Dogs—Fiction. |
Adventure and adventurers—Fiction. | World's Columbian Exposition
(1893: Chicago, Ill.)—Fiction. | LCGFT: Action and adventure fiction.
Classification: LCC PZ7.M36354 Am 2016 | DDC [Fic]—dc23
LC record available at https://lccn.loc.gov/2016018799

10 9 8 7 6 5 4 3 2 1
First Edition

For Pamela,
who brought us together

CONTENTS

Anton and Cecil
Cats Aloft

The two kittens flopped down on the warm brick apron outside the lighthouse at Lunenburg and batted their paws at the slim orange cat sitting nearby.

"Tell us a story, Kitty!" shouted Mo, the smaller of the kittens.

"What kind of story would you like?" asked Kitty, smoothing her whiskers with one paw.

"One of Anton and Cecil's adventure stories," said Sophie, settling next to Mo. "A scary one, where they go far away!"

Kitty nodded. "The best kind. Your big brother

1

Cecil always told me, 'There are three ways to travel a long distance, and I've managed all three.'" She swished her tail jauntily just as Cecil would have done.

Mo lifted a paw. "Oh, I know this! Across the sea by ship, over land by train, and . . . what's the third one?"

"Through the air, by balloon," said Kitty, gesturing toward the sky.

"A balloon!" cried Mo. "That's what *I* need."

"Tell us the balloon story," said Sophie. "Please."

Kitty cleared her throat and curled her tail over her front paws. The kittens scooted a bit closer while the cool fall breeze shook the leaves and pitched the ships in the harbor.

"The story begins," said Kitty theatrically, "with an ending."

CHAPTER 1

Out of the West

Where could he be?" wondered Hieronymus, rubbing his pink mouse ears. "I know my cousin is here *somewhere*. The mouse network said so!"

Cat brothers Anton and Cecil exchanged a small smile. Anton knew that the mouse network could be unreliable, but he didn't want to upset his good friend Hieronymus. Finding a tiny mouse in a giant city was as knotty a problem as finding a particular fish in the whole wide ocean. Anton and Cecil had found lost creatures before, of course, including Hieronymus himself, once imprisoned in a dusty railroad town, but this was no small town. This place was huge, sprawling over steep hills, tentacled like an octopus. Packs of hungry dogs and territorial rats threatened at every turn, and the local mice gave hazy directions. The cats and mouse pressed on, chasing down leads, scouring the port city from the sewers to the rooftops. After three sleepless days and nights, they finally found cousin Eponymus living underneath a food and drink establishment near the wharf.

"Oh, upon my last whisker, I thought we'd never find you!" cried Hieronymus, squeezing Eponymus with joy.

"And *I* thought we'd never eat again," growled Cecil, turning his attention to the scrap pile behind the saloon.

Upon their joyous reunion, the two mice swapped stories of their travels and trials, recalled their many now-deceased relatives, and discovered that they shared a fondness for fine salted nuts, stargazing, and lengthy conversation.

"Let's set up shop, shall we?" said Hieronymus to his cousin one bright morning as they sat on a weathered dock near the seaport. "We could meet the ships as they arrive and offer our advice as guides to all of the weary and bedraggled mice who disembark. What do you think?"

Anton, dozing in the warm sun nearby, awoke with a start. "You mean you're thinking of staying here?" he asked Hieronymus. "Permanently?"

Eponymus clapped his paws. "This is a brilliant plan! We could explain the ins and outs of steamboats and trains for those who yearn to travel inland."

"And we could connect them with the mouse network for help as they go," added Hieronymus.

"We could suggest places to eat and sleep."

"And places to avoid, don't forget that part . . ."

"It does sound like a valuable service," Anton agreed.

Hieronymus stepped over and grasped a pawful of Anton's fur. "I quite like this place, Anton," he said. "And with my cousin here, I could make it my new home." He paused and looked up at the storm-gray cat. "You could stay, too, you know."

Just then Cecil bounded up from the docks, the odor of fish surrounding him like a cloud. He flopped down in the grass with a huff and began to clean his white-tipped black tail.

"I don't know what it is," he grumbled, "but

the crabs out here can't compare to the ones back home." He shook his head. "Puny, stringy, tasteless things these are. And the fish are different, too. No herring at all, and I can't find a decent catfish to save my lives." He looked out over the port, then turned to Anton, his golden eyes flashing. "And it's awfully warm here most of the time. Have you noticed that?"

Anton stifled a smile at his brother's tirade. "I *have* noticed that, now that you mention it."

Cecil leaped up to all fours. "Are you as tired of this place as I am? I say we head back home for a bit. Check in on Sonya and the kits, tuck into some real port grub, eh? What do you think?"

The mice turned to Anton, their whiskers twitching, waiting along with Cecil for him to say something. Anton hesitated. Hieronymus was a true friend. He had once saved Anton's life aboard a derelict ship, and Anton and Cecil had undertaken a long and perilous journey to rescue him from a little girl's cage. But Anton was homesick, too, and his brother had a talent for getting into trouble. The new mouse plan would make it easier for Anton to leave; Hieronymus was happy to stay. He knew Cecil wanted to be on the move soon,

going anywhere—that was Cecil's nature—but finding home again would be tough, maybe impossible.
He didn't want Cecil to go alone.

Anton gave Cecil a firm nod. "I say blow that
whistle, brother. When do we leave?"

Cecil whooped and danced a little jig on the
dock. Anton sent Hieronymus a rueful smile. The
mouse clasped his tiny paws together, and Anton
knew he understood.

☆ ☆ ☆

The strange, sail-less wheel boat sat at the dock
like a waterfowl on the calm harbor, waiting to
shove off. In its shadow, Cecil lifted his chin in
salute to Hieronymus while Anton bent to touch
noses and bump heads with the small gray mouse.

"Farewell, my good friends," sniffed Hieronymus,
wiping his eyes with his tail. "Happy travels, safe
travels."

"Don't worry about us," said Anton. "And don't
forget to keep in touch on the network."

"All right, goodbye now," called Cecil, shoul-
dering Anton down the dock. "Good luck, you two.
Come on, Anton, let's catch our boat."

The last of the passengers had boarded and
the cats lingered as a dockworker closed off the

gangplank entrance with a rope slung across two posts. As soon as he turned his back, Anton and Cecil ducked under the rope, dashed up the plank, made a sharp turn under a line of deck chairs by the starboard bow, and disappeared into the shadows. The engine groaned as the giant bladed wheels on either side of the boat began to turn, slowly paddling the water like great oars and sending up a fine spray.

"Can you see them?" asked Cecil, crouched next to a large trunk and squinting at the noise.

Anton peered through slats in the railing and caught a glimpse of two tiny figures scampering away from the dock, headed toward Eponymus's alehouse home. "Yep," he said. "I see them." He watched the dock a little longer, frowning.

Cecil glanced up at him. "He'll be fine, you know."

"Oh, I know he will," said Anton, settling behind a chair and curling his paws under his chest. "It's us I'm worried about."

❖ ❖ ❖

When they'd first traveled over land by train, the brothers had followed the tracks "into the land of the setting sun," as Hieronymus had advised. Now,

Anton thought, it would be easy to reverse direction by heading toward the *rising* sun. The first part of the journey was obvious enough, anyway. A short distance up the road from the harbor where the wheel boat docked was a large train station, and since it was the "end of the line," as they'd heard it called, there was only one way to go: back the way they'd come.

"How shall we choose which train?" asked Anton as the two cats watched humans climb into a particularly long set of carriages. Two engines linked together, one before the other, chuffed at the front like powerful draft horses.

Cecil shrugged. "Doesn't matter, does it? They all have to go the same way out of here."

Anton stood up and paced. "Maybe we should be strategic about it. We could pick a shorter one that might zip along like a baby snake." He sat down again. "Or perhaps the longer ones go farther down the line before turning around."

"You're overthinking it," said Cecil, yawning.

"Maybe we should avoid the passenger trains altogether." Anton rubbed his chin with a paw. "Those humans never seem to like loose animals riding with them."

"I believe this one is a fine choice," said a small, tinny voice from behind a tuft of grass.

Cecil tensed, ready to spring. "Who's there?"

"I'm Felix, sir, from the mouse network, here to advise you about your train selection," the voice continued, though its owner did not reveal himself.

"Huh. And why should we listen to you?" Cecil asked, pointing a paw.

Anton shushed Cecil and spoke toward the grass tuft. "So you think this one's okay, do you?"

"Oh, yes, sir," came the thin voice. "Your needs will be well met on this train. Our advice is to board the second-to-last carriage. Just ignore the cage of pigeons you'll find already stowed there."

"Ignore it?" said Cecil, smacking his lips. "Sounds like lunch to me."

"Ho, very funny, sir," said Felix. "I'll be off now. Best of luck with your travels." A shiver in the grass, and he was gone.

"Well, what do you think?" asked Anton, still scrutinizing the train.

"We've got our orders, don't we?" said Cecil, his eyes twinkling.

Anton smirked. "Since when do you take orders from a mouse?"

"I don't. But I thought you might. Let's go!" Cecil bounded to the second-to-last carriage and, hardly pausing to make sure Anton was following, slipped inside. They were underway once again, at last.

❖ ❖ ❖

Anton and Cecil hid among the boxes in the carriage, keeping well out of sight like the stowaways they were, until the train pulled away from the station and began picking up speed. Then they crept out and sat by the partially opened door, gazing at the passing scene. Anton found himself almost enjoying the return journey. The cragged mountains and steep, shadowed valleys were familiar even in their strangeness. He recognized a few of the small towns where the train stopped to take on and leave passengers, and the cooler air made the trip in the stuffy carriage bearable.

The cage of pigeons turned out to be high entertainment for Cecil. They were carrier pigeons, being transported to a place in the wilderness where humans were gathered. Cecil couldn't get at the birds through the bars, but he spent many hours quarreling pointlessly with them all the same.

"Our job is to ferry messages from the field back home again," explained one chubby bird, strutting importantly. "With all of the distances we've traveled, I'd say we are the world's greatest explorers."

"Oh, please," Cecil scoffed as he lounged against one wall of the carriage, his tail flicking lightly on the floor. "Being a carrier pigeon doesn't make you a great explorer. You fly from point A to point B with a scrap of paper clamped to your leg. That's not *traveling*."

The biggest of the pigeons hopped indignantly in the cage, well out of Cecil's reach. "Of course it's traveling!" she howled, red eyes bulging. "We see the world. We fly tirelessly for miles on end. We rely only on our wings, and the stars, not on any man-made contraptions."

"What's this you're on, then?" Cecil countered. "And what's that you're locked in? It's shackles from start to finish, my friend."

The pigeon stamped her clawed foot. "The train only takes us where we are needed. On the return, we fly freely in the sky. We could leave at any time we choose."

"Could you?" asked Cecil, sitting up and gazing at the pigeon curiously. "Could you go against your instincts and veer off the path? Hmmm?" The bird huffed and the cage burbled with anxious cooing.

"Cecil, stop torturing them," said Anton from

the doorway of the carriage, where he was following their progress across dizzying mountain bridges and through narrow passes. Cecil stood and stretched, then joined him at the door. Anton lowered his voice. "You're asking for deep thoughts. They're just birds, after all."

"I guess you're right," said Cecil, "but I *am* envious, in a way." He glanced back at the cage. "I'd love to fly."

Anton chuckled. "With your girth, brother, you'd better keep all of your paws on the ground."

❖ ❖ ❖

The landscape sloped into gentle foothills as the train rambled on toward the rising sun. The cats were able to quiet their snarling bellies by sniffing out scraps or pilfering snacks from unattended baskets at stops along the way. But the train didn't stop at every station, and Anton could tell by the way Cecil eyed the pigeon cage that he was hungry.

On the morning of the third day, the train pulled into a busy town set on the flat plains and surrounded by fields of tall prairie grass. The cats peered out at the bustling scene.

"We've been here before," said Anton.

"Yep, and there's the place where the engine

turns around," Cecil observed, nodding toward a roundhouse off to one side behind a gate.

"That means we have to get off and wait for a train going the right way," Anton said.

"Plenty of time for a snack, then." Cecil jumped down from the carriage and darted toward the town buildings with Anton on his heels.

They waited all that day for another train to arrive, and dozed through the night. By the following morning the cats had found plenty to eat but were growing restless. They circled the town warily, alternately watching the humans, other animals in the streets, and the tracks. When Anton finally heard the shrill whistle of an engine, he ran to the station. A short train stood ready to leave, headed in the direction they wanted to go, but Cecil was nowhere to be found.

"Cecil!" Anton howled. "The train!" No answer.

Anton sprinted through the station and into the main town road, dodging cart wheels and horse hooves. "Cecil!" he cried again, then rotated his ears, listening. Where could Cecil be that he wouldn't have heard the train?

A burst of laughter spilled from an open doorway on the next block. Anton lifted his head and heard players and singers banging out a thumping music from within. He hurried to the door, took a deep breath, and plunged inside. His eyes adjusted to a riot of swinging dresses and stomping boots, and he crept low against a wall, scanning the floorboards for his brother.

Anton spotted Cecil's white-tipped tail sticking out from behind the bar and dashed to the spot. Cecil's head popped up, his face smeared with red-brown sauce, a small pile of meaty bones under his paws.

"Hey!" Anton called over the music. "The train is here."

"Good timing!" Cecil said with a smile. "I was just finished."

The two cats bounded through the saloon and into the street. Another whistle pierced the air, followed by the slow, plodding chug of a train beginning to move. Thick white smoke billowed from the engine as Anton and Cecil rounded the corner of the station at a run. Anton pulled up short with a cry. The doors to the carriages were all shut—there was no place for the cats to stow themselves.

"The back end!" shouted Cecil, galloping ahead. "We'll have to jump on!"

A short set of iron steps led up to a narrow platform at the rear of the very last carriage. The engine was gathering speed, chugging faster, and humans at the station shouted and pointed as the cats sped down the tracks, chasing the train. Cecil reached the steps first and vaulted aboard. He crouched on the platform as Anton tried to catch up.

"Come on, come on!" Cecil called. "Grab ahold!"

Anton flung himself onto the first step, his paws slipping on the dusty metal, his tail dragging along the rails and swinging dangerously close to the grinding wheels. And then he was up and pitching side to side as the train shimmied on the tracks.

"You made it!" Cecil grinned at Anton, who was still wide-eyed with fear. They crouched and leaned against each other to steady themselves, and together they watched the station fade into a haze of dust behind them. The little platform was coated with a film of smoky grease and dirt, and the wheel racket was deafening. The carriage rattled and clacked, shaking ceaselessly for mile upon mile.

"This is worse than traveling in the hold of a ship," grumbled Anton.

"Nonsense!" cried Cecil, wincing at the squeaks coming from under the train. "We're out in the fresh air." He sucked in a dusty breath. "And it's a better view than we usually have."

Anton glared at him. "You're impossible."

Suddenly the door to the carriage burst open and a young man with a blue cap stepped out onto the platform. He gripped the rails and surveyed the landscape for a few moments, then turned and put one boot on the bottom rung of a metal ladder that led up to the roof of the train. He began to whistle a tune but stopped when he caught sight of the cats, huddled against the carriage wall and staring bleakly at him. *This is it,* thought Anton miserably. *He's going to throw us right off.*

The man paused, his fingers tapping the ladder railing, and then smiled and continued to climb. The brothers exchanged a glance, and Anton sighed with relief. A lucky break.

Shortly after that, it began to rain.

⁂

The train rumbled in a straight line across the vast prairie, sweeping past stations and barreling on through rain showers and gusts of wind. The man with the blue cap returned and set a large bowl of milk on the jouncing platform. The cats lapped it up in short order, but the man did not invite them inside the carriage, and Anton and Cecil were left huddling against the chill as the miles rolled past.

By late afternoon the sun had returned and the cats' fur dried and warmed a bit. Houses began to appear on either side of the tracks, some with fenced areas penning horses or cows. Soon humans appeared, walking or riding in horse-carts, and larger buildings loomed behind them.

"We must be coming into a town," said Cecil. He crept stiffly to the side railing and stuck his head through, peering ahead toward the engine.

"A big one, from the looks of it," said Anton.

"Very big," agreed Cecil.

The train slowed to a crawl, and stationary carriages appeared on other sets of tracks alongside the one the cats traveled on. After a long curve, the train chugged slower still, and then a shadow passed overhead as the engine glided into a massive covered station. There was a loud clanking from the front, then a sharp hiss, and the train jerked to a stop. Anton and Cecil scrambled down the steps and looked around the station.

"Well, that's the end of that," said Anton, lifting

his chin toward the solid back wall, against which all of the engines were nosed in and silent as if napping.

"So what now?" asked Cecil. "Where are we?"

They trotted to the giant open end of the station and gazed out. Before them lay a maze of tracks, twisting away in all directions, and beyond the tracks was an immense body of water, glimmering in the afternoon sun.

"I don't know," said Anton. "That's not the ocean, I don't think. It doesn't smell right. We must have slept through this station on the way out. I can't see where to go from here."

Cecil turned toward a long boardwalk where humans traversed in a throng. "Where there are people there should be animals," he said. "Let's go talk to somebody."

CHAPTER 2

Ruby

"The thing I notice," Cecil said, as he and Anton made their way through the crowd at the enormous station, "is that when we came out this way from home, the mouse network was nowhere in sight, and now every time we stop, they're all over us with advice we don't need."

Anton chuckled. "There you go, brother," he said. He pointed to a trio of mice, straightening their whiskers and puffing out their tiny chests, who were waving to them from under a luggage cart.

Cecil groaned. "It just takes the fun right out of it for me."

"They mean well," Anton reminded him. "And this station looks pretty confusing."

Cecil dodged a passing boy who was tugging a suitcase as large as he was. "It's big all right," he agreed.

A tall lady pulling a struggling puppy pushed between the two cats. "I just want to go home," the puppy whined. "Why can't I go home?"

Anton watched as the lady and her pet moved on through the crowd. Across the platform he saw another dog, a big female, not young, leaning against an iron rail with her nose pressed to the ground. She appeared to be on her own. *That's unusual,* Anton thought, but his brother distracted him.

"Those mice are going to wave their arms off," said Cecil.

Indeed, the three mice were still waving vigorously and the biggest one squeaked, "Mr. Anton! Mr. Cecil!"

"At least they get our names right now," Cecil observed.

"Let's go see what they have to say," Anton said.

Cecil led the way and the mice pressed together,

whispering into one another's ears. The heaviest mouse, who had a bold, confident manner, stepped forward and began his address.

"Welcome, welcome," said the mouse. "News of your journey runs ahead of you, and we are all bound to assist you in any way we can, for the service you rendered our brave fellow Hieronymus, and especially for your fine work in discovering his whereabouts, and freeing him from captivity."

"Yes, right, of course," said Cecil, gawking all around, his nose wriggling.

Anton nodded to the mice. "This is the biggest station we've ever seen," he said. "We know we have to change trains here but we're not sure which one to take."

"And we could use a meal before we set off," added Cecil. "That last ride was long and wet."

As Cecil spoke, Anton glanced past him and noticed the big dog again, loitering near a newspaper stand, this time sitting back on her haunches with her head raised in the air. What a face she had, as long and gloomy-looking as a rainy day, and her ears were huge heavy flaps that hung down well past her chin. Her eyes were closed, but as he watched, they opened and focused on him.

"We'll escort you to your track," the officious mouse assured them. "You're heading for the sea, correct? That would be the train with the red stripe down the side, if I'm not mistaken."

A thin, elderly mouse next to him cleared his throat. "I believe you *are* mistaken, Frank. The train to the sea is the one with the green stripe."

"I'm sure it's red, George," the heavyset mouse corrected, still smiling at the cats.

The third mouse, quite young, shook her head. "The sea train is black, all black, and fearsome."

The mice fell to bickering about the train, and Cecil rolled his eyes. "You three work this out, will you?" he said. "We'll find something to eat in the meantime."

The first mouse nodded, shushing the others. "There's a good fish restaurant just down the block and they throw the heads in a bin at the back door—it's a favorite place for the local cats, so of course, we'll only take you to the corner."

"Sounds great to me," said Cecil.

"It's been a long time since we've had a chat with a local cat," Anton agreed. He looked toward the staircase and there was the dog again, half-hidden by the curving rail and clearly staring at the cats.

"If I'm going to meet city cats, I want to wash my face," Cecil said, and he sat down, bringing his paw to his mouth and smoothing his whiskers and forehead.

"A dog is watching us," Anton said to Cecil, lifting his chin. Just as Cecil followed his gaze, the dog came out from behind the stairwell and strode directly toward them, her mouth open, drooling a little as dogs do to the everlasting disgust of all cats. But most notable was this dog's nose, which was large and quivering. She hardly looked at the brothers as she made her way smoothly through the crowd—she was definitely following her nose. The mice bunched up, though they didn't appear to be afraid.

"Don't worry about her," said the young mouse, waving a paw. "She's eccentric, but a friend to all creatures. She's quite well-respected in the dog world, we hear."

When the dog was very close, she lifted her head and closed her mouth, working her loose lips as if tasting the air. Cecil cast Anton a skeptical look as the dog addressed them in a gravelly voice.

"Excuse me, gentlemen," she said. "I wonder if you would be so kind, that is, if I might have a word with you."

"We're new here," Cecil said coolly. "We can't give you directions."

The dog fluttered her eyes at this response and Anton thought she looked amused.

"Oh, dear me, I know you're new here," said the dog. "You see, I would, wouldn't I, because I am rather old here. I'm here a great deal. And I thought when I saw you that you are certainly new here, which got my attention, but what I especially noticed, and what struck me as really very odd, if you don't mind my saying, was that although I felt certain that you've never been here before, well, I couldn't help but notice that you were talking with a trio of our local mice. And that just struck me as so unusual, if you get my meaning. One so rarely sees travelers of your kind, actually on their own, as it were, as it appears you are, but even if one did, they are pretty unlikely ever to be having a conversation with mice."

The cats stared in wonder at the sheer number of words this huge dog had just strung together.

Cecil nodded. "It's a fair point. We've actually talked to plenty of mice lately. And now we're talking to a dog, which we've done before as well. What kind of cats are we? I ask myself that every day."

"You're the brave, canny, detective kind of cats," the biggest mouse piped up. He turned to the dog. "They've traveled this land from sea to sea, following difficult clues and using their wits to free our comrade from a terrible fate. These two are the famous brothers Anton and Cecil, known to mice everywhere. If you've lost a friend, they can find him."

"Is that so?" said the dog. "Well, I'm pleased to meet you, though I haven't lost a friend. My name is Ruby, but my partner calls me LeNez. And as for detection, it is a particular strength of mine. In fact, I'm something of a professional, though I won't blow my own horn. I'm in this station on a case, but I've determined that the culprit isn't here."

Anton looked around at the endlessly moving mobs of humans. "How can you tell in this crowd?"

"I caught his scent at the scene of the crime about a month ago, and it's not here today."

Cecil took in a good sniff. "I don't see how you can be sure."

"Of course you don't, my dear. But my nose is far superior to most. I have ascertained, for example, that you"—Ruby turned to the smallest mouse—

"had a bit of apple for your breakfast, and that you"—
she turned to Anton—"have brushed against a rubber
tire or perhaps a child's ball, yes, I think that's it, a
rubber ball, sometime in the last half-day."

Anton and Cecil exchanged looks of frank
amazement. They had skirted two children playing with a ball on a platform that very morning as
they ran for the train, and Anton had slipped by
just as the ball bounced, glancing against his side.

"So," said Cecil. "What did this culprit do?"

"It was a bank heist. Stolen goods. A lot of that
inked paper involved. It's not hard to track the
paper—acrid stuff, literally burns the nostrils, if you
know what I mean. We've come close to catching
him a couple of times now, really very close. But
our man is a dandy and he keeps changing his
shoes, which doesn't make it any easier. He smokes
a pipe, I've got that pipe down, and he smears a
particular flowery scent on his skin. It all adds up."

The mice snuffled, pretending their noses could
find anything but cheese, but Cecil stepped closer
to Ruby. "So what are you doing here today?"

"Well, my partner has decided that our best
course of action is to stake out the station—that is,

of course, to keep a watchful eye on it. The thinking, I believe, is that the culprit will likely leave town this way. My partner is counting on my picking up the scent, bless his heart."

"And who is your partner?" Anton asked.

Ruby lifted her chin toward a short man in a tall hat with a walking stick, who was in conversation with a young woman next to a long counter where another man served cups of something hot. "That's him. He's charming that young lady. The ladies do fancy him so. They call him Morgan or sometimes Mister Morgan. We've been together since I was a pup. Neither of us is as young as we were, but he's in his prime and has a great reputation, largely thanks to my efforts. Poor fellow, he can't smell a thing, and he's not too good with directions either. Keeps going through the wrong door, that sort of thing. But he's smart. He always knows when I'm on the trail and gives me a free hand."

Suddenly there was a bustle of humans near the tall glass doors that opened to the street. Several travelers, both men and women, entered the big hall. Some appeared to be together, some carried cloth bags or leather cases. They all looked ahead, seeking their destinations, but they had not gone far when Ruby took in a sharp sniff, swerved around on her haunches, and let out a soft bark. Her partner turned from the young lady, spotted Ruby, and, setting his cup down quickly on the bar, headed toward her.

"Our man is here," Ruby informed the cats. "Gentlemen, you're about to witness an apprehension." She got to her feet and strode off toward the doors.

Anton and Cecil looked at each other, and Anton cocked his head. "What do you think?" he said. The mice had retreated under their cart—Ruby's bark, though soft, had alarmed them.

"Sounds like fun to me," Cecil said.

Ruby was walking purposefully, her nose down, through the crowd. Her partner fell into step behind her.

"We'll catch up with you later," the lead mouse called as Anton and Cecil, shoulder to shoulder, stepped out to follow the man and the dog through the unknowing crowd in the station.

Moving smoothly, Ruby closed in on a tall, middle-aged man with a white silk cravat at his throat and shiny black shoes on his narrow feet.

Between his teeth he held a curved black stick that looked to be aflame, and he gripped a large leather satchel in one hand as he moved through the station, his eyes darting from side to side. He tipped his hat toward a passing lady.

"Is that him, you think?" Cecil murmured to Anton. "I notice he has no hair on his head."

"And one of his shoes squeaks," said Anton, his ears swiveling. "Hey, we're pretty good at this."

Ruby's head snapped up as the tall man passed her, and she spun to follow him. Mr. Morgan, her partner, took the cue and gestured with two fingers to a pair of young men in matching blue uniforms who were leaning against a nearby turnstile. The men each gave a slight nod and began walking in his direction.

Morgan stepped into the path of the bald man. "Excuse me, sir," he said with a genial air. "Might I have a word?"

The bald man removed the black stick from his mouth, pausing a moment while he took in the short man in front of him and the large dog, now alongside and sniffing the cuff of his trousers. His eyes narrowed and cut over to the two uniformed men advancing through the swarm of people.

"So that's the culprit?" Anton asked, craning his neck to watch the standoff. "He looks guilty."

"You can't tell by how they look," Cecil responded. "You have to see how they act."

At that moment the bald man blew a gust of smoke into Morgan's face, whirled, and bolted away through the crowd. Morgan coughed and stumbled forward, catching Ruby's eye and pointing, and the big dog turned and leaped after the bald man. Anton and Cecil jumped up to follow.

"*Now* he looks guilty," said Cecil, skirting around a cart loaded with trunks. The bald man burst through the double glass doors and out to the sidewalk, knocking other travelers out of his way. The cats caught up to Ruby just as she was buffeted back by the agitated crowd. She backed up, lowered her great head, and shoved through the doors with the two cats in her wake. Outside, the bald man was nowhere in sight.

"Oh no, he's gone," said Anton, disappointed.

"Not at all!" Ruby sniffed the ground and swung to the right. "This way!" she called, and the three creatures dashed down the street. Behind them, Morgan and the two men in blue tumbled out of the station door in pursuit. The sidewalk was busy with pedestrians, but most stepped to one side for the large dog as she hurried by, head down and nose working. Anton and Cecil jogged alongside, keeping a lookout for the bald man.

Cecil slowed at a side street. "Hey, the thing he had in his mouth—it's this way!" he called.

"The pipe, yes," Ruby agreed, veering quickly. The group sped up and then stopped short—the pipe lay on the sidewalk, ashes scattered. "He tossed it away to throw me off," Ruby huffed. "Nice try, but it'll take more than that to lose Ruby LeNez." She lowered her head again and took in two great nosefuls of air, then set off at a rapid trot. "I'll have to concentrate on his flowery smell. That and the trousers."

Anton looked back and saw Morgan and the others as they rounded the last corner, trying to keep the bloodhound in sight. Ruby scrambled down streets and alleys, pulling up short and doubling back, her nostrils flaring. The cats kept pace while trying to stay out of the way. As they passed through a quiet park, Anton thought he heard a familiar sound, faint and distant, but then he lost it again. They came upon the bald man's hat tossed to the side of the road, and then his scarf, but still not a glimpse of the man himself.

"He's going to have no clothes left by the time we find him," said Cecil, chuckling.

Ruby and the two cats arrived at a busy intersection and began weaving between horses and cart wheels in their path. A loaded wagon careened down the street, nearly running them over, and they were jostled and bumped on all sides by humans rushing along. Halfway across, Ruby stopped next to a lamppost and lifted her head, swinging her abundant jowls from side to side.

"All right, my friends," she said to the cats. "There are many satchels and a great deal of the acrid paper here."

Anton gazed around and was surprised to see that the street was indeed full of men similar to the bald man in one way or another, bearing hats and bags and cravats and even pipes, walking in every direction. The cats pressed in close to Ruby.

"Does that mean we've lost him?" asked Cecil.

"The trail is unclear," said Ruby, "and now I'm counting on the two of you. Think now. Do either of you notice anything?" She panted calmly as the seconds ticked by.

Cecil stood and paced, peering down each street. "I've got nothing."

Anton lifted his head and sniffed, but it was hard to concentrate with so much commotion. He shut his eyes and pricked up his ears, and he heard the sound again—a slight, repetitive squeaking.

"The man's shoe!" he shouted. "I hear it. Beyond that building." He jabbed one paw at a large structure in front of them.

"Excellent! Quick now, down the street!" called Ruby. "There will be an alley just behind."

Dodging a team of horses and a mob of ladies in crinkly dresses, Anton and Cecil raced the length of the building and around the corner to a narrow alley entrance, with Ruby close behind. The cats barreled into the alley, running directly under the feet of the bald man as he hustled toward the opening. The man stumbled and fell to one knee, dropping his leather satchel. The satchel bounced on the ground and burst open, emitting a cascade of small pieces of green paper that fluttered and settled across the pavement. Struggling to his feet again, the man reached for the satchel.

"Stop, thief!" Ruby barked at the man. She turned to check that Morgan and his crew were still following, then placed her substantial bulk between the bald man and the satchel, growling a warning to him. The man slumped heavily against the alley wall, his arms raised in defense, grumbling and cursing.

"Bravo, gentlemen!" Ruby said to the cats. "That was very well done."

Morgan arrived with the men in blue uniforms. After ensuring that the thief was well in hand, he came over to Ruby, who sat in the lane outside the alley with Anton and Cecil. He rubbed her neck affectionately and spoke to her with a certain pride in his voice.

"Good girl, LeNez," he said quietly. "You've done it again. What a marvel you are." He straightened and regarded the two cats curiously, smiled, and strode back into the alley.

"I don't know what he said, but your partner seems nice, for a human," Cecil observed.

"He has always been kind to me," agreed Ruby. "Though he's not so nice to the bad guys, I'd have to say." She turned to Anton with a twinkle in her droopy eyes. "That was a superior observation you made back there about those squeaky shoes."

Anton remembered how precise Ruby's sense of smell was. "You didn't really lose the man's scent, did you?"

"Perhaps not," she said, smiling. "But I *was* interested in what *you* might sense if you put your mind to it, and you heard that tiny squeak! My hearing's not what it was, that's true. And it's become a hindrance to me in a number of cases where I really need to be at my best." She looked from cat to cat. "I don't suppose we could consider keeping this team together a little while longer, could we? Mr. Morgan and I have been trying to solve a case over at the Fair that is absolutely confounding the both of us." She paused, watching them.

"Go on," urged Cecil.

"What's a Fair?" asked Anton.

Ruby smiled knowingly. "The Fair is a wonder of the world where humans of all types gather to listen to strange and beautiful music, to eat all kinds of delicious food, and to see sights nobody has ever seen before."

"Really?" Cecil's eyes were wide.

"Oh, goodness, yes. There's a giant wheel that spins in place, great halls and statues and fountains, and balloons that carry people into the clouds."

Anton nodded. "What's the case?" he asked the dog.

Ruby scratched one floppy ear with her hind

foot, and her face fell into its usual glum expression. "It's a troubling case that involves animals," she said slowly. "Animals being stolen from their families, whisked away without a trace, and no one seems to know where they go."

Anton and Cecil exchanged glances. "Well, we happen to know a bit about that kind of thing," said Anton carefully.

"Do you, now?" Ruby cocked her head. "That would be most helpful indeed, I'm sure it would. Tell you what." She stood and half-turned. "I'll go check on my partner for a moment, and you two discuss the matter. If you decide you're interested, I'll show you around the Fair and tell you more about the case." She tromped to the alley and stuck her head in, tail wagging lightly behind her.

Cecil glanced sidelong at Anton as his belly rumbled. "Did you hear the part about the food?" he asked.

"And the music," added Anton.

"And the balloons," said Cecil.

"And even the poor, stolen animals. The whole thing sounds like our destiny." Anton hesitated. "But what about going home?"

"We'll go," Cecil promised. "Soon as the mouse

network figures out how to get us there." He paused, smiling. "Remember those pigeons?"

"Yes, what about them?" Anton asked, wondering what his brother would think of next.

"Well, we've tried the sea and the land," Cecil mused. "Maybe this time we'll have to fly."

CHAPTER 3

A World of Wonders

As they followed Ruby along the busy street, Anton's and Cecil's eyes widened at the enormous looming arches of the entrance gates to the fair. On the other side, everything was bright, massive, and white. Humans passed in and out in great clutches, talking and laughing and pointing this way and that, and Cecil's ears swiveled at the din. He gazed up at the huge dome of a building in the distance, flanked by thick rows of columns on either side. There was a giant gleaming wheel, laden with swinging boxes as big as train carriages, that seemed to brush the clouds.

The wheel rose beyond a large pool in which a boat drifted aimlessly, and beyond that were more bright white archways just ahead, through which Cecil could see and smell water. But it wasn't the ocean—his nose agreed with Anton on that point. *Not a thing wrong with my nose, actually,* he thought, glancing at Ruby, who was leading them through the crowd. *And I don't have to put it on the ground to smell what's in front of me.*

"What is that water out there, Ruby?" Cecil asked. "It doesn't smell like the ocean."

"Your nose is correct, Cecil," replied Ruby. "That's a lake. Very large, but not as big as the sea."

"Jumping cats," said Anton next to him. "Will you look at the size of that deer? And it's white."

Cecil looked up and saw a deer twice the normal size, with a full spread of antlers, tip to hoof, powder white, and standing as still as a tree trunk on a big block of stone. Cecil was so impressed that he walked up and addressed the creature. "Mr. Deer," he called up to him. "What are you doing up there? Are you stuck?" The deer didn't move a muscle.

"I don't get it," Anton said.

Ruby, looking back over her shoulder, chuckled.

"It's a statue," she said. "Haven't you seen one before?" She turned herself in her tracks and joined her new comrades. "It's made out of stone. There are a lot of them around here. Humans never tire of admiring them."

"Oh!" said Cecil, nodding. "We *have* seen them before, but they're always of humans, never of animals. That's just weird."

"I do find it disturbing myself, I won't deny it," said Ruby.

"Do they have any of cats?" Anton asked.

"Not that I've seen," Ruby replied. "But there are more inside the buildings and I haven't explored every one. I do know where there's a statue of a fish, and right behind it there's a place humans eat clams and fish."

"Now that's a useful statue," Cecil said. "The sooner I see that one the better."

Ruby led the way again, not nose to cobblestone, but as confidently as any dog who knows where she is going, head up, tail sweeping slowly back and forth. Cecil looked this way and that, taking in the sights. The crowds were thick in some areas, thin in others, and there were a good many children, and ladies, many accompanied by dogs on leashes. There were no cats to see or to scent. Birds flew overhead, lighting on the various buildings or on the heads of the many statues, some of animals Cecil recognized: horses, a bear, two big moose, such as he'd seen blundering out of the woods in Lunenburg when he was hardly more than a kitten. He wondered if the statues were meant to capture the animals—to freeze them in place so humans could get a good look at them.

Cecil noticed that no one approached Ruby or shooed her away. In fact, he saw one of the men who had assisted in the apprehension of the thief, leaning against a chair with wheels, nod as Ruby trotted by. *I'd never want to be a dog,* Cecil thought. *Who would?* But if you had to be a dog, Ruby definitely had the human problem nicely solved.

The dog in question took a sharp left just past a huge statue of a female human, tall as a ship, standing on a block of stone out in the pool of water. Unlike all the others she was as gold as the sun, holding her arms high, perhaps in welcome. Cecil stopped to gawk at the strange sight just as the humans around him were doing. Anton looked back at Cecil and called, "Keep up."

"I'm coming," Cecil said. A familiar, briny scent

was floating toward him from a small building around the bend. He picked up his pace and as he joined his brother, they both let out a cheerful meow. There was a big statue of a fish standing on his tail. A carved seagull perched precariously, his stiff legs and sharp claws gripping tight, right on the top of the fish's head. As they passed the monument, the gull suddenly flapped his wings and opened his big bill.

"You'll be sorry," he said.

The intoxicating smell of fish—not cooked, but fresh—filled the air. A less enchanting sound accompanied the scent, the screaming of gulls, lots of gulls.

"Drat," Anton said, as he trotted past Ruby, who sat on her haunches, thoughtfully observing the pandemonium behind the food stall.

Cecil followed his brother and let out a huff of disappointment.

Before them was a small wooden platform jutting out over the water. On the platform a human boy stood at a wide shelf nailed to the top of a split-wood fence, a sharp knife in one hand, a silvery, gleaming, delicious-looking fish in the other. Next to him was a big hamper filled with more fish.

Before him, shrieking and flapping, rising and diving, nearly attacking him as he worked, a crazed flock of seagulls competed for the scraps. The boy threw the innards, heads, and tails into the air as he cleaned the fish, working fast to keep the big birds at bay. Now and then a bird came in so close he raised his knife to fend it away.

"How are we supposed to get any?" Cecil said disconsolately.

"Dibs, dibs," screamed the gulls. "That one's mine. Get back. Hey, don't hog that piece, that's a big piece. It's mine."

"Maybe if we get close to that boy he'll slip us a bit," Anton suggested.

Ruby came up behind them. "I believe the boy is not pleased to have such a greedy audience for his show," she observed. "In my view, if you see what I mean, he might welcome some relief." And with that she approached him. He threw a fish tail into the air, stowed the cleaned fish in a basket under the shelf, and turned to his hamper for another. Anton and Cecil followed close at the big dog's heels. The boy looked up and grinned widely at Ruby.

"Hey, old girl," the boy said. "What are you

doing out here?" He put the fish down and reached out to pat Ruby on her broad back. Anton and Cecil had no idea what the boy was saying, but he appeared very pleased by their visit. "You're sure a big girl," the boy said. Then he spotted the brother cats, who took their places on either side of the dog, endeavoring to appear deserving of fresh fish. "Look at that!" he said, his eyes wide. "Are these friends of yours? I never seen the like of that."

Unlike the boy, the gulls weren't pleased at all, and their screaming turned from squabbling among themselves to demands for attention.

"Get the dog out of here!" one cried. "Cats, get lost. This is our catch, go find your own." One bold bird swooped in very close and attempted to peck Cecil's neck.

In a flash Ruby leaped up, barking with sudden, fierce anger. "Leave my companion alone, you lazy scavenger!" she shouted. Then she showed her teeth and lunged, catching a feather or two as the astounded gull pulled up and, thrashing his great wings, rejoined his fellows. Ruby rushed to the very edge of the platform, rising up to rest her big forepaws on the fence and in a thunderous voice that the brothers hardly recognized, barked, "And stay back, you fiendish rapscallions, as long as I'm here. If you come close, I will bite your heads off. Do not dare to test my mettle. Let this boy do his work and wait your turns!"

The boy was ecstatic. "All right, all right!" he shouted. "Keep those darn birds in the water where they belong. You can stay as long as you want." He reached into the hamper, pulled out a fish, and hacked off the head and the tail. "Here you go, kitties," he said. "Any friend of this lady's is a friend of mine."

Cecil grabbed a tail, lots of meat at the front, and swallowed a big bite. Delicious. Ruby came back and sat near the boy, looking pleased with herself. *What an amazing old lady,* Cecil thought.

Another tail hit the wood and Anton nudged it toward the dog. "Would you care for a bit?"

Ruby widened her eyes, lowering her muzzle to have a closer look at the offering. "That's so courteous of you," she said. "But I had lunch with my partner at the station earlier. And, truth to tell, I'm not a great fan of raw fish."

"This one is too small," the boy said, pulling a fish the size of his hand from the basket. He slapped it on his board and cut it neatly in two pieces. "Just right for you fellows." And he tossed the waiting cats a perfect lunch.

"Let's eat here every day," Cecil said, as he pounced on this unexpected treasure.

"I'm so glad you gentlemen are enjoying the Fair," Ruby said. "It's a very cheerful place, to be sure. But sadly, as so often happens, there are those who take advantage of relaxed vigilance to do harm. And that's where I come in."

"Right," said Cecil, swallowing a meaty bite. "The case."

"When you've quite finished your luncheon, I'll go over the details with you. It's a most curious problem and we will need all the wits we have to solve it."

Anton licked a bit of fish scale from his lips. "You said animals are involved," he observed.

"Yes, puppies," Ruby said softly, as if she didn't want to be overheard.

"Puppies?" Cecil said.

"Small white dogs, from all over the Fair."

"What happens to them?" Cecil asked.

"Well, that's the mystery," Ruby said sagely. "We don't know what happens. They simply disappear without a trace."

❖ ❖ ❖

As the trio headed away from the lake and their delicious fish lunch, Cecil thought that Ruby was certainly right about the wonders of the Fair. He had never imagined buildings could be this immense, tiered and spired ever upward, or that so many humans would want to pack themselves together into one place at one time. The wide cobblestone avenues wound past shimmering fountains surrounded by trees planted right in the walkways without dirt or grass. Cecil's nose quivered, taking in scents of exotic animals he could not name, roasted meats and baked bread, leather, metal, fresh water, and the chalky white stone that made up every wall and column around them. He could see that the people were happy and excited, though the commotion was a bit overwhelming for a cat. He longed for a hidden alcove from which to observe the action.

Anton must have felt the same way. "I'm going to get stepped on for sure," he murmured.

Ruby led them on a path through a large plaza, around a central body of water she called "the Basin." Out on the blue water, men stood upright in skinny boats and ferried passengers slowly to and fro, steering with one long oar.

Cecil frowned. "If the pond is so small you can walk around it, what's the point of rowing a boat on it?"

"Ah!" Ruby looked back and smiled. "A good observation. It's just for fun, I believe."

"Going nowhere in a boat is fun for them?" asked Anton.

"Oh goodness, yes. Like fetching a ball thrown by Mr. Morgan, again and again, merely for the enjoyment of it." Ruby sighed.

The brothers exchanged a glance. "Well, that explains why no one seems in any hurry," said Cecil, skirting a group of raucous children blocking the middle of the lane. Just past the group stood a small clutch of men dressed identically, their backs straight and noses held high, watching the crowd in silence with shifting eyes. The men each wore a dark jacket with a column of shiny buttons down the front, and on each man's chest was pinned a silver star-shaped badge. One of the men touched the brim of his tall, round-topped hat at Ruby as they passed.

"Who are those guys?" asked Anton, hurrying to keep up with Ruby's loping strides.

"Those are the police, standing guard to protect

the people from theft, assault, and other crimes and tomfoolery," replied Ruby quietly, raising her great head to survey the men.

"Is there a lot of that kind of thing here?" asked Cecil, eyeing the guards over his shoulder.

"More than you would imagine, my dear."

Just as the trio stepped into the shade of a small tree, a sharp bark pierced the din of the crowd. "Ruby!"

The three companions turned toward the sound and watched as a small, elegant dog sidestepped the pedestrians and headed for them at a fast trot, her paws a blur. Her curly white fur, stark against the black clothing of the humans, had been clipped short along her torso and legs, leaving puffy balls near her feet and around her head. A braided leather leash encircled her narrow neck and trailed behind her. She glanced at the cats for only a second before nosing in to the group, a look of panic on her pointed face.

"You're Ruby, the great detective, aren't you?" she asked the older dog, speaking rapidly.

"Yes, my dear," replied Ruby. "Camille, is it? We met a few days ago."

The white dog nodded distractedly. "I need

your help!" she cried out. "My son, he's gone!" She wobbled on her skinny legs. "He's disappeared, and I don't know where to turn!"

"Oh, heavens," Ruby exclaimed. "I'm so sorry. Now, try to calm yourself a bit and tell me exactly what happened." Ruby touched Camille's nose with her own and stood solidly near the dog's shoulder as she composed herself. Anton and Cecil took a few steps backward into the shade and crouched, listening intently.

"That's just the trouble! I don't know what happened." Camille glanced at the crowd behind her and took a quick breath. "I don't have much time. My owner is looking for me, but I had to try to find you right away."

"Indeed, and I do hope I may be of service. I am working on this very case, if your situation is as I fear." Ruby nodded grimly. "But the details, please. Give me what you remember."

"Yes, all right," said Camille, lifting her cloud-like head. "We were walking on the Midway—my owner, my son Jasper, and me. My owner stopped to watch several humans dancing in a circle outside an open tent. The dancers were waving colorful cloths through the air, and there was music. A big crowd had gathered and we were standing toward the back, so Jasper and I couldn't see very much. My owner was apparently taken with the show, so we lay down on the ground on either side of him to wait." She paused, shaking her head.

"Go on," urged Ruby gently. "You're doing fine. This is all quite important."

"It happened so fast. Someone stepped on my tail and I yelped and jumped up, and when I turned back Jasper was . . . just . . . missing!" A sob caught in Camille's throat. "I immediately started barking to get my owner's attention. I looked around but I couldn't see anything in the crowd. Ruby, I know what you must be thinking, but he wouldn't run away, not from me."

"No, of course not, my dear. Now let me ask you. Do you recall picking up any particular scents at the time?" Ruby looked dubiously at Camille's petite nose.

Camille shook her head sadly. "Not in particular, but there were so many human smells in the air, it was confusing."

Ruby eyed the leather collar. "Was Jasper on a leash, similar to yours?"

Camille cocked her head. "Well, yes, he was," she said slowly, "but I'm not sure what . . ."

A commotion in the crowd made them all turn.

"Queenie!" a deep voice bellowed. "Queen of Sheba, where are you?"

"That's my owner," said Camille, a guilty look on her face. "I ran from him to find you." She turned and stepped into the roadway just as a heavyset, bearded man burst through. His face was red and perspiring. From one hand, another leather leash dangled, empty.

"Oh, Queenie!" cried the bearded man, dropping to one thick knee. "Come here, my girl. I thought I'd lost you as well!" Camille trotted to the man and allowed him to rub her neck and shoulders affectionately. Ruby, moving quietly and quickly, circled behind him and sniffed at the leash that looped on the ground beside him.

"You've made a friend, I see," said the man, scooping up the handle of Camille's leash as he rose to his feet. He patted Ruby's head and then nudged her away. "Come along, Queenie. We'll find your pup, not to worry. I understand there's a detective here who's top-notch. Morgan's the name, I believe. This way." He strode off down the path with Camille, who turned and sent Ruby one last pleading glance over her shoulder. Ruby returned a deep nod.

"Well!" she exclaimed, returning to the shade of the tree where Anton and Cecil sat pondering what they'd just heard. "That was a breakthrough, of sorts."

"Was it?" said Anton. "How?"

"Was it a clue about the missing puppies?" asked Cecil.

"*Stolen* puppies, to be more precise," said Ruby, gazing dolefully at Cecil. "At first we did consider them to be merely missing, Mr. Morgan and I. Mysteriously missing dogs. Perhaps lost. Perhaps runaways. We have, up to now, concentrated our efforts on locating these lost souls somewhere here at the Fair, but I'm having my doubts that this is a simple string of straying pups." She shook her head decisively. "No, I believe we are firmly in the realm of thievery!"

"What makes you so sure?" asked Anton.

"The leash that man was holding, for one thing," said Ruby. "Did you notice anything strange about it?"

"It was made of the same braided rope as Camille's," offered Anton. "I noticed that."

"It must have been Jasper's leash, but there was no Jasper at the end of it," added Cecil. Just

thinking about Camille's young son in this enormous crowd, all alone and scared, made his belly
ache. What if that were one of the kittens?

"Right on both counts," said Ruby approvingly.
"But the breakthrough was even bigger than that."
Her eyes were bright above her drooping jowls. "It
wasn't only Jasper that was missing at the end of
the leash."

"It wasn't?" said Anton. "Well, what else could
be missing?"

"The collar was gone as well," explained Ruby.
"The leash had been cut!"

"Cut!" repeated Cecil. "So that means somebody intentionally took Jasper, right?"

"That would be my deduction as well, Cecil. A
finding that turns this case on its ear."

CHAPTER 4

The Ice Railway

"Gentlemen, I think we should split up."

Ruby sat in the alley next to the narrow house she lived in with her partner, Mr. Morgan, while Anton and Cecil lapped up milk from two small saucers. On their way back from the Fair the previous evening, Mr. Morgan had turned to see the cats trailing behind Ruby. When he got home, he brought a dish of food out to them in the alley where they'd tucked themselves inside a tipped-over crate. The food was some kind of canned fish, salty and sour, but the cats were grateful. Ruby accompanied Morgan out with the milk the next morning, and stayed with them to plot the day.

"Split up?" said Cecil, licking drops of milk from his whiskers. "Why?"

"Yes, why?" echoed Anton. "The Fair is enormous, with so many humans everywhere."

"And that's exactly why we should split up, my fine feline fellows," said Ruby. "Divide and conquer, that's the idea."

"It sounds like you already have a plan," said Cecil, moving on to clean his face with one paw. "Let's hear it."

"That I do, and here it is." Ruby stood to pace a little as she talked. "First, I'll need to be on hand when Mr. Morgan speaks to the owner of the poodle who was snatched yesterday, as I may be able to draw a few more details from his mother, Camille."

Anton interrupted. "What's a poodle?"

"It's one kind of dog," Ruby explained. "A type. Camille is a miniature poodle."

Cecil looked at Ruby's long face. "You're not a poodle, are you?"

"Goodness, no," snorted Ruby. "I'm a bloodhound, descended from a long line of talented noses, I might add." She took a large sniff of air.

"Bloodhound, huh?" said Cecil. "Sounds intimidating. Are there lots of different types?"

Ruby nodded. "Very many, indeed. What kinds of cats are there?"

Cecil shrugged and rubbed his ear with a paw. "Well, some are slim, some stout, some all one color, some striped."

"Some are smooth, others fluffy," Anton put in. "We're all just cats, as far as any I've ever met."

"Well, my dear, that may change today," said Ruby, continuing to pace. "I want Cecil to go up to the Ice Railway and talk to a cat who is there every day with her owner. The owner is a stocky old woman who wears piles of animal furs draped over her shoulders." Ruby shivered with distaste. "The cat is an odd one—unnaturally thin, always tucked in the lady's arms, won't speak to me at all. She only ever hisses, the miserable thing, and that's about the extent of what I've been able to get out of her. But the pair of them have been around the Fair since it opened, and the cat may know something about the disappearing dogs. Something she might share with a fellow cat."

Cecil nodded thoughtfully. "The Ice Railway? What is that?"

"It's a track that runs in a circle, covered with snow. The snow is always there, though one never sees it falling." Ruby gazed into the distance, musing. "Quite strange, really. The humans ride around the track sitting in a cart, screaming and howling as if they are at wit's end with terror. Though they must like it well enough, as I observe a large crowd lining up to take the ride every day."

"Ought to be easy to find, then," said Cecil, standing and stretching. "An unfriendly, hissing cat. Okay, where should we meet, and when?"

"Let's meet near the fishing boy after our tasks, and we'll share what we've learned," said Ruby.

"Wait," said Anton, "what am *I* doing?"

"Of course, Anton, I'm not forgetting you," said Ruby, turning. "You should go to the animal show. The humans call it the Menagerie. There's a show every few hours that features several performing creatures, though it takes place inside a building that I've never been allowed to enter." She swung her head around, her long ears flapping. "I'm just too big, I suspect. At any rate, animals who work at the Fair may have superior inside knowledge of the crimes, so I'd like you to sneak in somehow and speak with them."

"How will I know which place is the Menagerie?" asked Anton, rising to join Cecil.

"It's on the Midway, near the Ice Railway, where your brother is bound," said Ruby, tilting her head toward Cecil. "You'll know it by the five lions in cages outside the door."

"Lions?" said Cecil, his golden eyes widening.

"Biggest cats you've ever seen, I'll wager." Ruby winked at the brothers. "All right, let's get to work."

Cecil thought of the Great Cat, Montana, a huge, solitary creature they had met in the mountains, far behind them now. Montana would never, ever be found in a cage. Who could these strange big cats be?

✼ ✼ ✼

The Midway was a long, straight thoroughfare, and no cat could see from end to end with all of the jostling, crowding humans in the way. The humans probably couldn't see very well, either. Compared to the more placid areas of the Fair over by the Basin with the frozen, white statues posing here and there, the Midway's sounds were a cacophony of chatter and music, the air pungent with strange cooking and animal hides and overheated people. And the sights! There was a novelty every time Cecil turned his head. Colorfully dressed dancing ladies, their wrists and fingers flashing in the sun; strolling creatures twice as tall as their human riders—big as bison but light-colored, skinny-legged, and hump-backed; a man wearing a length of cloth wrapped around his head for a hat, thrusting a flaming sword down his throat and then whisking it out again, smiling and bowing for the crowds. It was impossible to look away.

"Cecil!" called Anton. "Look where you're going!"

Cecil turned and found himself face to face with an enormous cat-like creature. The creature appeared to be sleeping, reclining in a squat, narrow cage with great black bars for walls and a few gnarled bones strewn in one corner. The animal's fur was tawny gold, and its pink tongue lolled out between pointed teeth as it breathed steadily. Most striking was its face, angular and regal, surrounded by a thick ring of dark brown fur that was long and wavy like human hair. Cecil froze, staring at the creature, and Anton crept up next to him, crouching low.

"Is this the big cat Ruby was talking about?" whispered Cecil.

"Must be," said Anton softly. "There are four more of them, see?"

Cecil glanced at the others, some dozing, some pacing narrowly in their cages. The cages were set on either side of the entrance to a large building. A man approached one of the other enclosures and spoke jeeringly to the big cat inside. The cat growled and sprang toward the bars, and the man jumped back.

A deep, hoarse voice came from nearby. "At least use the proper name, will you? We are lions."

Cecil and Anton stepped away from the cage, but the lion who had just spoken didn't move. He opened one yellow-brown eye and fixed it on them, still resting his head on his two massive front paws.

"What business do you have here?" the lion rumbled. He opened the other eye and blinked at them slowly. "And what are you, anyway, house cats?"

"Traveling cats, more like," said Cecil, watching the lion's tail, which was tufted with the same dark hair that surrounded his face, flick back and forth along the dusty floor of the cage.

The lion's eyes narrowed slightly and he lifted his head. "*Traveling* house cats. Hmph. Where have you traveled?"

"We've sailed in ships over the ocean," said Cecil, pulling himself up, "and we've ridden on trains all the way across the land." Anton nodded beside him. It did sound impressive, Cecil thought.

The lion evidently did not agree. "Not bad," he said, yawning. "The six of us came across the sea in a ship and then on a train to get here." He nodded toward the other lions. "It was awful."

"By my count there are only five of you," said Anton.

The lion regarded Anton coolly. "There is one more inside, little house cat. So, again, what's your business here?" A note of irritation had slipped into his voice.

"We are . . ." began Cecil, but then he paused. Would Ruby say it was all right to speak of their investigation, or was it top secret? This lion did not seem especially friendly. "We're looking into a mystery, to help a friend," he said.

The lion snorted. "A mystery, eh? Let me guess. Are you referring to the missing pooches?"

"*Poodles*, you mean," Anton corrected. "The type is called poodles. Have you seen anything?"

"No, I have not," snarled the lion. "As you can see, I don't get out much." He glared at the cats.

"I've heard the fuss being made about the whole mess, though I can't imagine why. The hounds probably just wandered off, is my guess. Wanted a little freedom, change of scenery. I can certainly relate to that." He stood up in the cage, and the small confines made him look even larger. "And who is this 'friend' you're helping? Don't tell me it's a dog, too."

Cecil nodded. "Afraid so."

"Working for a dog, looking for dogs. Pitiful." The lion shook his great head. "And you call your-selves felines. Well, there's a dog working the show inside, if you want more. A little high-strung, as they all are. Best of luck." The lion turned and slumped again, facing the other way. "And don't try the front entrance," he added over his shoulder. "They'll toss you out on your ear. Go around back."

"Thanks," said Anton, though the lion said no more.

Cecil stood and gazed around. "Well, you've found your assignment. Now I'm off to find mine. See you later." And with a swish of his white-tipped tail, he melted into the crowds of legs and feet on the Midway.

❖ ❖ ❖

The Ice Railway was hard to miss. Not only was it elevated high above the roadbed where the Fairgoers strolled, but it took up a space the length of three or four buildings lined up along the Midway. As Ruby had described, it was a giant looping track on which humans rode in open carriages shaped like horse-carts without wheels. And the carriages needed no wheels on the track, Cecil soon discovered, because they slid on a sheet of ice.

Cecil could feel the cold pouring off of the surface of the track in a wave as he approached. It felt good, especially as the sun rose and the day warmed. One end of the Railway was enclosed by a tall, windowed building, and wooden staircases led riders to the top floor on either side. *If I'm to get a good look at this thing and find this mysterious hissing cat, I'd better get up high,* thought Cecil, and up he climbed, dodging sharp toes and heels the whole way. At the top he slinked out onto a platform overlooking the track, settled himself under the railing, and gazed out.

Long, pointed flags whipped on tall poles overhead like the tongues of lizards, much bigger than the small flags on ships but without any pictures on them, only squiggles. At the far end of the ring stood a low building with a smokestack puffing out billows of black smoke in time with a loud, chugging engine. The carriages on the track had low, elegantly curved sides and were set on runners, like the sleighs horses pulled through the winter snow in Lunenburg. The ice sparkled as the morning sunshine lit the track. Of course, Cecil had seen ice on ponds and puddles during the bitter winters back home, but it melted at the first sign of spring warmth. He'd never seen such a thing in midsummer.

Great crowds of people waited to take a turn riding the sleigh around the ice track. A short set of steps led from the platform down to a smaller landing next to the track, where riders got on and off the sleigh. Cecil scanned the humans, whose faces mostly looked alike under their black hats, smiling and craning their necks to see ahead. One face did not smile, Cecil noticed. A short, thickset woman, her mouth set in a scowl, stood off in one corner of the landing and watched the riders with a brooding glare. She wore a layered coat, despite the warm day, and Cecil realized with a start that the coat was made from long swaths of animal furs stitched together as fabric.

That must be who Ruby was talking about, he thought, and rose to his feet to get a better view, ducking under the railing and leaning out. Sure enough, nestled in the crook of the woman's furry arm was the head of a very lean cat—a cat who appeared to have no fur at all.

Cecil was still focused on the strange woman and even stranger cat when a trio of boys climbed onto the bottom rung of the railing just above his backside, shouting and pointing at the whizzing sleigh below. When a woman in the line called to the boys, they jumped down from the rail in unison, one landing hard on the tip of Cecil's tail.

"Yeeeoooww!" Cecil screeched, leaping away. He scrambled to regain his balance but found himself tipping over the platform's edge, tumbling through the chill air, and dropping onto the ice-covered track below like a sack of flour.

Thunk. He landed on his feet but his paws immediately splayed out in all four directions, sending him down to his belly. *Ooof.*

Cecil lay still for a few seconds, gasping to recover his breath. He stared ahead at the steep downhill run, his underside beginning to numb. The Fair-goers who had seen him fall were causing a commotion, some squawking, some tittering with laughter. Cecil glanced over his shoulder, his head spinning, and saw the hulking sleigh poised at the top of the run, held fast by ropes as the passengers stepped inside and settled into their seats. His heart jumped—the sleigh was almost full. It was exactly as wide as the track and was kept aligned by rails on each side. As soon as the ride workers unwound the restraining ropes, the sleigh would begin its run around the track.

The sleigh was aimed directly at him.

I've got to get out of here, and quickly, he thought, and began scooting down the track on his belly. When that proved to be entirely too slow, he popped out his claws, dug into the ice, and dragged himself upright. *I'll jump off the track, easy as pie.* Wobbling precariously over to one side rail, he glimpsed the long drop to the ground and skidded to a halt. *That's no good.* He turned and looked at the empty, ice-covered track ahead and gulped. *Then I'll have to outrun it.*

The ride workers untied the ropes holding the sleigh steady and it began to move. A few people on the platform above waved and shouted, "Hey! Cat! There's a cat on the track!" but the workers didn't hear them in the din of the crowd. More people joined in, yelling helplessly as the sleigh gathered speed, bearing down on the solitary cat.

Cecil scrambled on the ice, trying to find his balance and gain traction with his claws. He began to make slow, clambering progress, skidding and sliding. He found a rhythm and moved faster in leaping bounds. The crowd hummed with confusion and excitement.

Sprinting to the top of a tall rise in the track, Cecil threw himself down the other side, flopping to his belly again and trying to stay low. Ice crystals flew up into his eyes and nose as he barreled down the track. He could hear the sleigh behind him, its runners crunching the ice as its weight sent it careening along.

Cecil's heart raced. *If I can only get back to the landing, then surely the men will throw out the ropes to stop the sleigh.* But he was losing hope that he could outpace the huge carriage. Wheezing, his eyes misting and his nose running, Cecil risked a glance behind. The sleigh sped down the hill and was gaining on him. One more low hill remained before the finish. Cecil looked back once more to gauge the height of the sleigh's runners, then sprang up the low hill with all his might.

The crowd had whipped itself into a frenzy, shrieking with fright and cheering him on. His muscles ached; his ice-covered paws felt like lead. He heard the hiss of the sleigh as it drew still closer, and he hauled himself over the top of the hill with the last of his strength. Just past the peak, he dropped to his belly on the track, pressed himself as flat as a stout cat could get, and held his breath. The giant sleigh whooshed over him and thundered down the hill.

The crowd gasped and murmured as Cecil lay on the ice, dazed. After a few moments, he dragged himself up and began staggering to the finishing area behind the sleigh. The Fair-goers erupted in cheers and applause.

"He's alive!" they shouted. "Bravo, Ice Cat! Hail to the Ice Cat!"

A man rushed toward him and Cecil knew he should try to run, but he had no strength left. The man held a large blanket and scooped Cecil up carefully, using one corner to wipe the ice from his ears and whiskers. Cecil tried to squirm away but the man swaddled him in the blanket and carried him to the side landing, directly to where the sour old lady in the fur coat stood, watching them approach.

The lady clucked her tongue. "All that fuss over a tubby tomcat." She eyed Cecil and wrinkled her nose. "Is the creature alive?" she asked the man, who nodded and set Cecil down on the wooden planks of the landing with a final swish of the towel. The lady sniffed and turned away to watch the next sleigh run. Cecil had hoped that the lady was telling the man to bring him something warm to eat, but that never seemed to be what humans talked about. He shook out his fur and licked his paws to thaw them, ignoring the stares and calls of onlookers in the crowd. He felt bruised and dizzy, like he'd rolled down the side of a very cold canyon.

"Quite a show, that was," hissed a female voice nearby. "Do you always crash a party like that?"

Cecil looked up, his neck aching with the effort. The hairless cat was peering at him over the old lady's elbow, a sneer on her peculiar face. Her eyes were round and pale yellow, and her ears were huge, bat-like, sticking up high over her pinched face. The cat's head and shoulders seemed thin and frail, perhaps because she had no fur. She had wrinkled folds of skin, like a human's, a patchwork of soft pink and smoky gray. This was the cat that Ruby had told him to talk to.

Cecil pulled himself up, though it pained him. He lifted his chin toward the track. "It's a pretty good ride, but I wouldn't go again, I don't think."

The hairless cat crept a little farther out of her burrow in the coat as the old lady stroked her oversized ears. She smiled smugly, revealing a row of needle-like teeth. "*I* wouldn't have gone the first time. Who *are* you, anyway?"

"I'm Cecil." He flashed her a grin. "Visiting from the land of the rising sun. Just passing through on my way home. And who are you?"

"My name is Zuma, though my mistress calls me . . ."

"Jellybelle, quiet," said the sour woman, patting Zuma on the head with thick, bejeweled fingers.

Cecil ignored the woman. "And you're a kind of cat, right?" he asked carefully.

Zuma's smile tightened. "Of course I'm a cat. Just like you. Well, not *just* like you. I'm part of a pure line descended from the Aztecs, whereas you're a common alley cat."

Alley cat? So I am a type after all. Cecil couldn't resist asking Zuma the obvious question. "Don't you get cold, hanging around the Ice Railway with no fur?"

Zuma's smile faded altogether. "Never. I'm perfectly warm in my mistress's coat."

Cecil gazed at the coat and grimaced. "You do realize, don't you, that it's made of fur?"

The hairless cat shrugged. "Not cat fur."

Cecil was tiring of this unpleasant creature.

"So, do you and your mistress and her coat stand up here often?" he asked.

Zuma sniffed and inclined her head regally toward the track. "We are here every day to watch the races. My mistress brought the great ice-making machines from New York City for the Fair."

"The ice is quite a wonder," Cecil agreed. "So if you're here every day, you must know a lot about what goes on."

"Of course," replied Zuma. "I see *everything*."

"Jellybelle, hush, will you please?" The old woman glanced down at Cecil, then turned her broad back to him and took a few steps toward another corner of the landing.

Cecil followed, trying to stay out of the woman's line of vision. "Zuma?" he called quietly.

After a pause, Zuma stretched her skinny neck over the folds of coat and glared. "Shhh," she hissed at Cecil. "Go away. You'll get me in trouble."

Cecil's eyes widened. "In *trouble*?" He shook his head. Being a pet sounded like a worse deal all the time. "Okay, I'll leave. Just tell me—do you know anything about the dognappings that have been going on? Have you seen anything?"

A flash of fear lit Zuma's pointed face for a moment, then she half-closed her eyes and sank into the coat.

Cecil moved around to one side of the lady to try to see Zuma again. "What is it? *Do* you know something?"

Zuma burrowed into the crook of the woman's arm, and her voice rasped out from underneath the woman's elbow, directly down to Cecil. "You're a perfect stranger here," she said almost in a whisper. "How do I know it's safe to tell you? You could be working for him."

For him, thought Cecil. A small clue. "No, I'm trying to solve the mystery," he said. "My brother and I are working with Ruby."

"Ugh, the bloodhound." Zuma heaved a sigh, muffled in the fur coat. "It's so frightening. I worry constantly that I might be next."

"Why would *you* be next?" asked Cecil. "You're a cat."

"Yes, but they surely know my value," Zuma insisted. "I'm quite rare, you know."

Cecil saw an opening and nodded. "You're right," he said, pumping concern into his voice. "A well-bred cat like you *would* be a prime target. If only we knew more about the culprit, we could protect you . . ."

The old woman huffed and began to stride from the platform. "Honestly, Jellybelle. Haven't I told you about consorting with this kind of ruffian? It's beneath you." She shifted her arm and the hairless cat disappeared.

Zuma said no more as she was carried away. Cecil trailed behind the pair down the outside staircase to the ground level. The woman whisked open a door leading into a room full of people and good smells, but Cecil wasn't going to be fast enough to get in after them.

"Zuma!" Cecil yelled up. "If you know anything, help me!"

As the door began to swing shut behind them, Zuma stuck her head back up and hissed at Cecil from over the woman's shoulder. "There's a man with a mustache who wears a sporting cap. He's the one cutting the leashes!" The woman reached up and grabbed the folds of skin on the back of the cat's neck to tug her down again, but Zuma struggled against her to spit out one more piece of information. "His cap. It's greeeeeen!"

And the door slammed in the frame, leaving Cecil outside alone.

CHAPTER 5

The Menagerie

Anton thought he could probably slip through the front entrance to the Menagerie, but as he drew closer, he saw two of the police officers Ruby had told them about scrutinizing the crowd. He remembered the lion's advice—don't go in the front door. Better sneaky than sorry. He veered around to the back of the building, where he found an open window, a little too high for a human to see into, but with a wide sill just the right height for a cat to leap up on. With a couple of steps back to get the angle right and a concentration of his muscles . . . boom,

Anton landed squarely on the sill. Then he let out a gasp of surprise.

He was looking into a strange world indeed, and he was free to stare as all eyes were on the animals running and leaping and cavorting round and round a dusty circular track. Anton watched the ring through a wide opening between two ranks of raised seating.

A horse with an elegant blue cloth draped across his back cantered near the edge while a lion loped alongside, and a medium-size furry black dog brought up the rear. In the center of the ring, a woman in a red dress and hat snapped a whip over the head of the horse, and stood, speaking forcefully to the lion. The lion was an older female, Anton observed, without the thick brown ruff of her friends outside, and she was muttering to the horse as they came round the aisle near the window.

"Slow down a little, and get your head down, would you?" the lion said. "The tamer wants me on now."

The horse whinnied and slowed, stretching his long neck out and lowering his big head. "I'm ready," he said. "On the count."

"One, two, three," the lion said, making a few

long strides between each number. On three, to the delight of the crowd and Anton's astonishment, the lion leaped up and landed on the horse's wide back.

The dog barked triumphantly. "Great job, Mala, you're up. Whoa, I'm next." The woman with the whip was tipping her hat, bowing right and left to loud applause.

A voice addressed Anton from just below the window ledge. "You must be the smallest lion in the world."

Anton dropped his eyes from the spectacle in the ring and gaped as he made out the impossible animal standing quietly in the shadows. It was no bigger than a large dog, but there all possibility of doggyness ended. The creature was covered in a pale gray, hairless, wrinkled hide, with legs droopy like stuffed human trousers, big flaps for ears, and, most alarming of all, a nose that hung down, down past his mouth in a long, flexible rope to the floor.

"A lion is a cat," Anton said, "and so am I. My name is Anton. But what in this world are you?"

"I'm a baby elephant. So I'm sort of like you, a little version of a bigger one. Are you going to get bigger?"

Anton hopped down to the sawdust-covered floor next to the elephant. "No, I'm fully grown."

"Oh, I'm sorry to hear that," said the creature, swinging her ear flaps. "When I grow up, I'll be so big I'll touch that roof up there." Anton glanced up at the high roof, almost invisible in the shadows, and nodded politely. The little elephant raised her long nose toward Anton, as if she wanted to sniff him. "They call me Lily, but my name is Pakadaka. Paka for short."

"Are you part of this show?"

"I do a dance at the beginning with Tommy, that's the horse, and another one at the end with Sparky the dog. But I don't go on with Mala, the lion. She's too grumpy. But just wait 'til I get to my full size. If she's mean I'll pick her up with my long, strong trunk and I'll fling her into a pile of hay. That'll show her!" She nodded firmly. "I've been working on my trumpeting, too. Listen." She raised her long nose, puffed out her cheeks, and blatted a loud, shrill call that sent shivers down Anton's spine.

"Well, I don't know what full-size trumpeting sounds like, but that's not bad," said Anton, turning to watch the ring.

The dog yapped cheerfully as he ran, "Here we go, here we go, I'm coming up. Are you ready, Mala? Are you ready, Tommy?" With an amazing leap, he landed square on the horse's hindquarters, then leaped again up to lion's back. The crowd burst into wild applause.

"Did you come just to see the show?" asked Paka.

"Not really," Anton replied. "I'm trying to figure out who's nabbing dogs from the humans who come to the Fair."

"I heard about that," Paka said. "Sparky is very upset about it. You should talk to him."

As Paka spoke, the ongoing act came to a close and the crowd stood up, shouting their approval. The lion and the horse went out a far exit, while the black dog trotted into the wings where Anton and Paka waited.

He greeted Paka gleefully. "Good house tonight," he said. "Really a live audience. Tommy was in great form." Then he noticed Anton sitting by the elephant. "Who are you?" he said. "Did you see the show? What did you think?"

"I'm Anton," Anton said. "And I did see the show. I thought it was amazing."

"Yeah. We were like a well-oiled machine out there. Smooooth as butter."

"Anton is upset about the little lost dogs," Paka told Sparky. "He says a bad person is nabbing them." She curled her trunk around and touched it gently to two pointed white stubs protruding from either side of her face. "When I get my full-size tusks, all bad people will run away screaming when they see me coming!"

"You bet they will, Paka!" said Sparky. Paka lumbered off to speak to Tommy, and Sparky shook his head. "She's what they call a pygmy elephant," he told Anton in a low voice. "She's not going to grow any bigger than this, but we don't have the heart to tell her."

"Wow," said Anton. "That's tough."

"I know, it is, but what do you know about this dognapper?" said Sparky anxiously. "I know something about it, but I can't do anything because I'm always working."

"I've been helping a dog who's on the case," said Anton. "Bloodhound, name of Ruby LeNez."

"Ruby LeNez!" the dog replied. "I've heard of her. Everydog's heard of her. She's a famous detective. She solved the Case of the Empty Yard. It just never occurred to the humans that a basenji could jump that high."

"That may be, but she's stumped on this case," Anton said. "Anything you know that will help us would be much appreciated."

"Right," said Sparky. He sat down and opened his mouth, panting a bit. "Promise to tell Miss Ruby that Sparky gave you this info, okay?"

"Definitely," Anton agreed.

"One of the first pups I heard about was nabbed right from this tent. I didn't see it happen—I was doing the show—but it was like this. The lights went out for just a moment and then I heard a lady shout. When they came back on she was wailing and her dog was gone. Now here's the thing I noticed." Sparky glanced around and leaned in toward Anton, lowering his voice again. "When I went into the ring there was a man sitting very near where she was and he had a basket alongside him—I noticed 'cause it was sticking out in the aisle when I ran in. But when the lights came back and all the humans were gathering around the screeching lady, the man and the basket had disappeared."

"Disappeared?" Anton repeated. "So you think the man put the pup in the basket?"

"It sure seems possible, doesn't it?" Sparky licked his nose excitedly. "And here's some more news. As we were coming round the bend today, I noticed he was there again."

"He's here now!" Anton exclaimed. "Where is he?"

"He's on the far side of the ring, just near the exit."

"I'm off," Anton said, and he rushed down the aisle.

Before he could enter the ring, two guards jumped out of nowhere and blocked his way, shouting, "Only show animals in here! Get back."

Anton turned and rejoined Sparky in the wings just as Paka trundled up. "How am I going to get over there?" Anton said.

Sparky frowned thoughtfully, and Paka snuffled her trunk in the dust. "Hey," he said. "I got a brilliant idea."

✤ ✤ ✤

The tamer snapped her whip at Mala until the lion jumped up on a big barrel off to one side, growling moodily. The audience grew restive in their seats. The tamer turned her back on Mala, gesturing toward the sidelines, and the final act began.

Sparky, Paka, and Anton dashed out into the

center of the ring while a steam organ struck up a lively tune. The tamer eyed Anton suspiciously, striding toward him with her hand extended. At that moment Paka stood on her hind legs and began to dance. Sparky ran merrily around her, barking and leaping, and Anton ran behind Sparky as if on a chase. The audience laughed, and the tamer paused uncertainly. When the elephant came down on all fours, the dog swiftly leaped onto her back, and the cat jumped up as well, landing easily on the dog's back. The elephant pyramid padded lightly around and around the ring.

All the while, Mala continued her growling. "What's a house cat doing in here?" she complained.

Anton could only glance at Mala as they passed closer to her barrel. He saw the lion stand and arch her back, her tail twitching. *Not good,* thought Anton. *She's getting worked up.*

"I've had it with this dumb show," the lion growled. "It's undignified. This is an outrage!" And on that last word, Mala roared.

The audience took in a collective breath of terror and the tamer turned on Mala, snapping her whip, but she was too late. The lion leaped from the barrel and came down facing Paka.

The poor little elephant slammed to a halt and screamed in terror.

Mala swiped at the cowering Paka, but Anton, sliding down her long nose, saw that the lion's claws were sheathed.

"She's just trying to scare you," he called to Paka.

Anton turned and hissed furiously at Mala. "All great cats are brave and noble. Where's your nobility?"

Mala growled but said nothing, still looming over Anton and Paka. Anton saw the tamer approaching, her whip raised. He whirled to Paka.

"Show her what you've got, Paka!"

Paka nodded fiercely and took a breath. Anton ducked just as she blared a high trumpeting note from her trunk, right into Mala's face. The lion flinched, grimacing, and scooted away.

Anton gave Paka a wink. "That sounded plenty big to me!" he said, and the little elephant grinned.

Sparky ran up, speaking quickly. "Hey, the dog thief is opening his basket," he announced. "He's over there, right next to a lady with a pup."

Anton swerved to follow Sparky's direction, and as he did the lights strung across the top of the tent flickered and went out. The audience screamed

with alarm but it wasn't pitch dark, and Anton's eyes adjusted easily. He had his eye on the man near the exit and he watched with dread as the man opened the lid of a fishing basket on his lap and deposited a fluffy white puppy inside. The man wore a scarf—a bright yellow scarf, unlike all the white collars and bow ties the gentlemen mostly sported. The man turned and made for the exit as the lights flickered back on. It was several moments before everyone heard two women shouting in dismay. Anton raced toward the exit on his trail.

"Tell Miss Ruby Sparky sends his regards," the dog shouted.

Anton ran past the tent flap so quickly the two guards only had time to call after him, "No cats!" Then he was in the crowd, darting among the human legs, intent on spotting the man with the basket. Anton looked up and down, this way and that. He caught a glimpse of the man's fluttering scarf through an opening where a side lane crossed the wider road, lined with tents and people. Anton dashed past a woman who was dressed in very odd clothing and dancing as if her feet were on fire. The fellow was moving away from the crowd along a narrow path. But how could a cat stop a man?

Anton redoubled his speed, but before he could close the gap, he first heard and then saw a great troupe of humans banging on drums they carried in front of them and blowing horrible racket out of shiny metal tubes of all shapes and sizes. *Boom, boom,* went the drums, *yowl, blare,* went the tubes, and the men all stayed close together, walking fast. They barged across the path, paying no attention to the gray cat who bobbed from side to side trying to get around them.

The noise terrified Anton, and he couldn't see a thing through the marching legs. When at last they passed, it was too late. The man had vanished and Anton couldn't even tell which way he had gone. Anton stood on the Midway uncertainly for a moment, shaken by the vision of the purloined puppy. Finally, without looking back, he took off at full speed to find Ruby and share his hard-won clue.

CHAPTER 6

A Bird's-Eye View

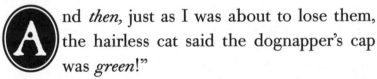nd *then,* just as I was about to lose them, the hairless cat said the dognapper's cap was *green!*"

Cecil, his expression triumphant, stood in the shade of a small grove of exotic palm trees, waiting for Ruby's response. He expected the canine detective to be over the moon.

Ruby, however, was silent, her long face pulled into an even longer frown than usual.

"Isn't that a great clue?" asked Cecil. "Most hats around here are black, right?"

"Well, yes, Cecil," said Ruby, shifting her big

paws uncomfortably. "Most human hats do tend to be as black as your fur, that's very true. And I dare say that the clue you have unearthed will do us a great service on this case. Yes, I'm quite sure it will. It's just that . . ." She paused, took a long breath, and finally sighed. "I don't know green."

Cecil stared for a moment. "What do you mean?"

"I mean, I don't know the color green, Cecil, simple as that," said Ruby, gazing at him levelly. "Dogs don't have green, as a rule. I've heard other creatures mention it, most particularly birds, who seem to see dozens of hues, but I can't say that I can distinguish green in my surroundings. I do know blue and yellow, black and white." She lumbered over, sat next to Cecil, and blew air out through her nose.

Cecil closed his mouth, which had been hanging open, and looked straight ahead. "Are you sure?"

"Well, let's have a test, shall we?" Ruby lifted her chin gamely. "Go ahead now, give me a for instance. What's green, that you can see?"

Cecil raised a paw. "How about the grass there, on the mound in the middle of the Midway? That's green."

"The grass is the same color as the road to me," said Ruby. "No different."

Cecil looked at Ruby's watery brown eyes for a moment, nodding slowly. "All right, what about the leaves in the strange trees above us?" He craned his neck at the high branches.

"The leaves blend seamlessly with the sky, when it's cloudy," explained Ruby, gazing up as well. "They are quite similar in color to the water in the Basin and your brother's fur, now that I think about it."

"Then it's official," said Cecil. "You don't have green." The big dog nodded stoically, and Cecil went on. "It's no problem, though. We'll let you know of any green hats we see. In the meantime, your nose can tell us everything else. Like what a mouse had for breakfast . . ."

Ruby smiled. "And when Mr. Morgan last had a bath."

"And who keeps changing their shoes," added Cecil. "Yep, everything else."

The dog and cat sat chuckling quietly in the shade of the trees, watching the hordes of people stroll by under the steady afternoon sun. Suddenly, Anton burst through the tide of legs.

"Hello, you two!" he exclaimed. "I come bearing a clue. The puppies are being put in baskets when they're stolen."

"Excellent." Cecil leaned in conspiratorially. "I found out that the criminal wears a green cap."

"A green cap," repeated Anton. "Hmmm."

Ruby cleared her throat. "You know about green, I take it?"

Anton turned to her, amused. "Of course. But the man I saw had a yellow scarf, and no cap. Maybe there's more than one of them."

Ruby nodded. "Quite possibly. In my conversations with Camille and others, here's what we've determined so far. The dogs being stolen are all of small stature and light coloration, of types known for their intelligence and agility. Six have disappeared, each one brought here by a visitor to the Fair."

The brother cats sat thoughtfully. Cecil curled and uncurled his tail. Anton, whose gray fur was covered with sawdust, began cleaning his shoulder with long licks. Ruby fell silent as well. As the humans continued flocking past, Cecil stated the obvious.

"To tell the truth," he said, "the Fair is too big

and there are too many people for us to check them all for green caps or yellow scarves and baskets. I don't think we have much chance of finding the criminal from down here on the ground."

"What are you suggesting, Cecil?" Ruby asked, watching the crowd.

Cecil thought of how far he could see from the top of the lighthouse in Lunenburg. "We need to get higher," he said. At that, the three creatures raised their eyes skyward.

"Into the trees?" offered Ruby.

"Up to the rooftops?" suggested Anton.

"Higher," said Cecil, lifting his chin. "How about on top of *that*."

Anton and Ruby followed his gaze across the road and up and up, to the tallest structure at the Fair—a gigantic wheel made of massive metal beams, spinning on an axle the size of a tree trunk. The top of it seemed to brush the clouds. From each spoke of the wheel dangled a boxy windowed carriage, the glass winking in the bright sunlight.

Cecil was surprised to see that each carriage was jammed full of *people*. "Humans will ride in anything, won't they?"

"Look who's talking," said Anton, giving Cecil a nudge.

"My partner calls it the Furs Wheel," said Ruby, squinting up. "The most popular place at the Fair, by far. People just adore riding in those boxes way up high and then down again, round and round in a circle."

"Have you ever gone up there?" asked Anton.

"Me?" said Ruby. "Heavens no. I'm pleased to keep my paws on the ground, thank you very much. I'm no climber like you felines. Besides, they wouldn't brook an animal in one of those fancy boxes for a second." She looked sidelong at the cats.

"Then we'll have to ride on top," said Cecil, turning to Anton.

"We?" said Anton, his eyes widening.

"Sure!" said Cecil, his whiskers twitching. "We can look for caps, and baskets, and all sorts of clues. We'll be able to see for miles."

"That's what I'm afraid of," said Anton.

⚜ ⚜ ⚜

Cecil and Ruby hustled Anton across the Midway and into the crowd in front of the Wheel. Each box on the Wheel stopped at a platform as it passed to let passengers on and off through doors on either end. The bottom of the great Wheel dipped below the platform on its way around.

"We can jump onto the top of one of the boxes down there, do you see?" asked Cecil, gesturing with his head toward the space below the platform.

"I do indeed," said Ruby, beginning to muscle her way through the multitude of humans. "Stay close behind me, then go when you can."

"I'm not crazy about heights," muttered Anton. The two cats crept up the stairway, keeping out of sight by tucking under Ruby's belly.

"It's important work, Anton," replied Cecil seriously. "We've got clues but we need the big picture."

Anton opened his mouth to protest further, but just then Ruby planted her paws and began a woeful and frightfully loud baying, her heavy jowls rippling with the effort. A space immediately cleared around her on the platform as the humans recoiled and stared, and the cats seized the chance to slip away.

"Quick, down here!" called Cecil. He dashed to the edge of the platform overlooking the deep lower arc of the Wheel, readied his front paws, and sprang lightly onto the roof of the nearest box. Anton hesitated only a second before following. The roof was peaked in the center, and the brothers flattened themselves against the far side of the peak, out of view of the Fair-goers. They had only a moment to settle in before the giant Wheel began to move.

A thunderous *chuff-chuff-chuff* issued with a cloud of steam from a tangle of pipes situated on the ground nearby, and the Wheel began turning on its axis. It rose smoothly until the box of humans ferrying the cats reached the platform, then stopped for passengers to enter and exit. Ruby's baying cries were subsiding now that her task was accomplished, and the excited chatter of the people below drifted up. With a slight jerk, the box began to rise again.

While Anton stayed as flat as he could on the warm metal roof, Cecil sat up and let the breeze fluff his fur. As the Wheel carried them higher into the air, Cecil swished his tail with delight.

"Isn't this incredible?" said Cecil, turning his head in every direction. "Look how far we can see! It's like flying!"

"But we're supposed to be looking for clues," Anton insisted.

Cecil glanced down at Anton. "You're going to have to sit up, then."

The Wheel stopped again for passengers with

a mechanical *thunk,* and the box swayed. Anton gulped.

"You're looking a little wobbly, brother," observed Cecil. "Come over here, breathe the fresh air. See? There's the Basin with all those white statues around it."

Anton raised up a little on his forelegs. "Oh, wow, I see it. And the boy with the fish who fed us yesterday, over there." He took a breath and steadied himself. "Look at those strange twisted trees—the huge leaves look like they could swallow you up."

"Ho, there's a little girl with a green hat on," said Cecil, looking straight down. "She's not a likely culprit. How about the other way?" He turned and stepped over the peaked roof to the opposite side. "I see a bunch of humans stacking themselves, one atop the next while spinning rings on their arms." Cecil shook his head. "Why do they *do* stuff like that?"

The Wheel began its mighty turn again, and up they rose. Every time the Wheel stopped and rocked, Anton stretched out his claws to grab something to hang on to, but the metal was flat and slick and he scrabbled along the warm surface.

He inched forward on his stomach and peered over the edge.

"Great cats above," Anton breathed. "I could never be a bird, that's for sure. Say, there's the balloon ride Ruby was talking about," he said, pointing a paw. "The two huge balloons resting on the ground, see?"

"I wonder how high they go," said Cecil. Anton didn't respond, and Cecil turned to tease him again. But Anton was motionless, his ears swiveled forward and his eyes focused on a spot far down the Midway.

"I see something else," Anton said softly. "Look out there, past the building with the curved roof, near where that boy is tossing things in the air and catching them. There's something green, isn't there?"

Cecil braced his front paws and opened his eyes wide. "Oh, hey, it's a . . . green cap," he said slowly. "A man with a green cap, but he's walking away so I can't see his face."

"Yes!" said Anton, with rising excitement. "Watch him and let's see where he goes."

At that moment, with a blast of steam from the engine, the immense Wheel began to turn once more, lifting Anton and Cecil higher in the sky. At the same time, two birds fluttered by overhead and landed on top of the passenger box just above the cats. They were unusually large, one more plump than the other, with eye-catching blue and yellow feathers, fringed tails, and long pointed beaks. Cecil had never seen birds like these before.

"Don't even look at them," Anton warned. "Stay focused on our job."

But Cecil was distracted. He twisted his neck to stare up at the birds, who perched on the edge of the box above and chattered away to each other, never looking down.

"I just think," said the plump bird, preening her chest feathers, "if they really want us to stay put on that dismal island so that people can gawk at us all day, they should stock the lagoon with better fish."

"Oh, quit complaining," said the thinner bird. "The parrots are stuck in cages over by the Basin. That'd be a whole lot worse." She flared out one brilliant wing, examining it.

"I hear you," agreed the plump bird. "But they get fancy seeds over there, plus crickets if they speak to the humans."

"Too much trouble." The thin bird shook her beak. "I'm glad we can fly, at least."

"Right, and we're not getting snatched like those dogs," added the plump bird.

The Wheel started up once more, and this time the birds' box rose to the top of the giant circle. Cecil paced along the roof of the cats' box just below, watching the birds intently.

"Did you hear what that crazy goose Mimi said about that, by the way?" asked the thin bird, strutting along the edge of the roofline. "She said that she was up at cloud level one day and she thought she heard dogs crying in the sky. Can you believe that?"

"Crying in the sky?" squawked the plump bird. "Oh, that goose is a loon, honestly." She chuckled.

"A loon, ha." The thin bird tittered and tapped the other with a wing. "Good one." She turned and noticed the cats for the first time. "Flying feathers," she screeched. "Felines dead ahead."

"Ugh," said the plump bird mildly, peering across. "I can't stand cats. But don't worry. What are they going to do, jump over here?" She turned her back and shook her tail feathers at Cecil.

Cecil stepped to the edge of the roof and hissed at the birds. Just as Anton opened his mouth to warn him off, the Wheel ground into motion again, this time without stopping. In a sweeping arc the boxes were carried over the top of the circle and down the other side. The birds sent a steady stream of taunts at the cats.

"You tough guys gonna fly and get us, or what?"

"Hey, fat cat! Stuck on a hot tin roof?"

"Gonna use up some lives, getting out of this one, that's for sure."

As the Wheel revolved, the birds' box descended underneath the cats' perch, and Cecil glowered down at the birds as they yammered up at him.

"Ignore them, Cecil," pleaded Anton.

"I can't endure insults from *birds*," Cecil growled.

At that moment the steam engine hitched and the Wheel jolted sharply as it revolved. The dangling boxes quavered on their hinges. Anton struggled to hang on, his claws spread wide, scraping the metal. Cecil, balanced on the far edge, yelped as the box jounced. His eyes met Anton's in terror as he slipped straight off into the air.

"Cecil!" Anton cried, lunging toward him. Cecil's front paws spun, grasping at the box desperately, and then he dropped like a stone.

Cecil flailed as he fell. *Clang!*—he crashed onto

the roof of the box below, skidded across the slippery metal and managed, barely, to stay on. He looked up, and for a brief moment he stared at the brightly colored birds only a few feet away, their beaks open in a silent squawk.

"Fat cat, huh?" said Cecil, and he lunged. Amid a flurry of shrieking the birds flapped away, spiraling unsteadily and hurling further insults as they went.

Anton's anxious face appeared over the edge of the box above, peering down at Cecil. Anton gasped, then shook his head and sighed with relief. "You're impossible, you know that?" he called down.

As the great Wheel carried them gracefully down and around and up into the sky, Cecil lay flat on his back, a pained grin on his face, a fluttery clutch of yellow and blue feathers in his claws.

CHAPTER 7

Balloon Race

ogs crying in the sky," mused Ruby. "Fascinating."

In the twilight of the day, the three friends had settled themselves in the alley next to Mr. Morgan's house. Cecil was banged and bruised after his two close scrapes at the Fair, and they all needed some rest and a good meal.

"Maybe," said Anton, lapping up the last of the canned fish and cream concoction that Mr. Morgan had brought out for Cecil and him. "Or, the birds could be mistaken about where the sound is coming from."

"Or they might be just, you know, wacky birds making stuff up," added Cecil, licking the scratches on his paws and belly.

"It's such a striking idea, though," said Ruby, gazing at the deepening blue above. "Crying in the sky. My goodness, what could that be about? Could it refer to the habit dogs sometimes have of crying *up to* the sky, baying at the moon, as it were? Because who among us hasn't done that, I might ask? Present company excluded, of course."

Anton frowned. "If the dogs are really *in* the sky, though, they'd have to be flying . . ."

"Which we know they can't do," Cecil put in.

". . . or up on something that's high itself," concluded Anton. "That puts us right back to a rooftop or a tall tree."

"Or the Furs Wheel," said Ruby. "No dogs to be found up there, I take it?"

Anton thought of the enormous contraptions he'd spotted from the top of the Furs Wheel. "What about the balloons?" he said, half-joking.

"They don't let any more dogs on the balloon ride than they do on the Furs Wheel, I'm sure of that much," said Ruby.

"What if they sneak on, like we did?" said Anton.

Just the thought of the swaying box at those great heights made him feel woozy again.

Ruby nodded, her ears swinging. "Anything is possible, as I've learned. And you did say that the man with the green hat was walking down the Midway, away from you, isn't that right? The balloon ride is down that way as well, so that's where we'll begin first thing in the morning," Ruby declared, standing and stretching her long legs.

"Can we go see the fishing boy first?" asked Cecil.

"Easily arranged," said Ruby. She strolled to the back door of the house and scratched softly at it. A moment later the door opened and a wedge of light spilled out, and Ruby disappeared inside.

"Well, brother," said Cecil, curling into a corner of the crate and resting his chin on his paws. "You ready for another high-flying mission tomorrow?"

Anton shook his head and sighed. "Not me. It was you who wanted to fly, you know."

"I know, and I know what you'll say, too." Cecil closed his eyes. "Careful what I wish for."

⁕ ⁕ ⁕

The rising sun warmed the air quickly and felt especially stifling to the furred creatures traversing the Fairgrounds. After a delightful breakfast thanks to the fishing boy and a stop at the Furs Wheel to get their bearings, Ruby, Anton, and Cecil began the slow work of navigating a path through the tide of humans, many of whom were streaming in the entrance at the far end of the Midway and clogging the main thoroughfare.

At a huge building with brightly painted walls and a soaring, rounded roofline, Anton pulled the others aside.

"This is about where the man in the green hat was, isn't that right, Cecil?" said Anton. He turned and gazed up to the top of the Furs Wheel, marveling at its staggering height.

"Somewhere along here, yeah," Cecil replied. "And there was a boy throwing things in the air and catching them, over and over."

Ruby nodded. "They call those people 'juglars.'"

"You know a surprising number of human names for things," observed Cecil.

"I suppose," said Ruby, scanning the hats in the crowd. "Mr. Morgan talks to me quite a lot, pointing at things and naming them as we meander about, and I have a good memory. If he identifies a thing or a person more than once, I usually can remember it."

"Is that useful?" asked Anton.

"Oh, very useful indeed," said Ruby. "Once, in a tight spot, he asked me to run to the butcher shop and get a leg of mutton—using human words, of course. And I did exactly that, and he was able to solve the case there and then."

"Wow," remarked Anton, turning forward again.

"Thank you, Anton. My thoughts exactly."

"No, I mean, wow, look at *that*!"

Through a break in the mass of people on the Midway, the group suddenly had a clear view of a grassy field next to the main road. There in the field, in front of a set of wooden stair-like planks filled with chattering humans, sat two enormous balloons, one dark green and one yellow. Their bottoms rested gently on the grass while the swollen spheres above listed in the breeze. From far away atop the Furs Wheel, the balloons hadn't seemed this immense. Standing below them now, Anton thought they were taller than the mainmast of a clipper ship.

"Look," said Cecil, gaping upward. "There's a Great Cat on each one."

Anton recognized a massive roaring lion painted on the fabric of the yellow balloon, and a strange, round-eared, striped cat, standing on its back legs and swiping the air, depicted on the green one. Each base was like a flat carriage, large enough to hold five or six humans, with low walls and a swinging door cut into one side to allow passengers to step in and out. A noisy machine chugged on the ground next to one of the carriages while a worker moved around it, adjusting the ropes attached to the balloon and arranging tanks and small crates.

"So, what happens here?" asked Cecil, eyeing the animated people seated on the planks. "Do humans ride in the carriages?"

Ruby sat down and nodded at the twin balloons. "They do. They call that bottom carriage a 'gondola.' Sometimes a balloon floats up and just hangs there, roped to the ground, and other times both balloons take off at once and sail away out of sight. I don't pretend to understand the rhyme or reason of it."

The three creatures circled around to the far side of the second balloon, away from the crowd on the planks. A small, dilapidated shed stood on the edge of the field, its door standing ajar. Ruby's nose began to wriggle.

"Oh, my goodness," she said, sniffing rapidly. "I'm picking up lots of puppy scents around here."

She moved carefully, nose to the ground, first toward the nearest balloon, then reversing course and heading for the shed. "More this way, I think. Let's spread out and search."

Anton and Cecil followed, their heads swiveling as they watched for signs of trouble. Ruby plunged into the shed while the cats circled around the outside. Against the back wall they came upon two small fishing baskets with rounded bottoms and flat lids. Anton cried out.

"The baskets!" he said. "These are just like the one that the man in the Menagerie had." He could hear Ruby inside the shed, knocking into things. He wanted to show these to her right away.

Cecil stepped closer and sniffed. "They do smell doggy, even to me." One basket was closed, its lid fastened with a loop of cord around a nail, but the top of the other was slightly ajar. Cecil wedged his nose under the edge of the lid and lifted it. "This one's not so bad," he said, his voice muffled. "Smells like there could be food in here."

"Food?" Anton repeated.

Cecil shoved the rest of his head inside. "Ah, here's a bone, a big one." He stuck his forelegs into the opening and, with a little spring off his back legs, he pivoted over the edge and disappeared into the basket. The lid snapped shut, the cord latch falling down over the nail.

Anton stared at the latch. *That's not good,* he thought. "Cecil, come on. This is no time for exploring."

The basket wobbled as Cecil moved around in the small space. "No meat left on this bone," he reported, sounding disappointed. "There's some damp cloth in here. It has an odd scent, makes my nose itch." Then he yawned loudly. "Goodness, I'm so sleepy all of a sudden."

"Come out, Cecil," said Anton. "I'm serious. Get out of there. It might be latched now—push on the top with your head or something." But Cecil had fallen silent. Anton stepped to the basket, nudging it with his shoulder. "Cecil?" No response. He stared at it, sighing with irritation. He turned and called through the wall of the shed. "Ruby? I could use some help."

Ruby's huge head appeared almost immediately around the corner. "What's happened?"

"Cecil's stuck in a basket." Anton gestured with a paw. "I think he's asleep. We've got to get him out."

"Remarkable," said Ruby, hustling over. "How does one even accomplish such things in so little time?"

"You don't know my brother," said Anton. "What do we do?"

"Well, we dump him out, is what we do," said Ruby. She lowered her head and bumped the basket forcefully. It tipped over on its side, but the latch held. She tried again, sending the basket tumbling, but the lid stayed shut.

Anton felt a little panic begin to rise in his belly. Someone was bound to notice them any minute. "Maybe I can bite through the cord," he suggested.

"Worth a try," Ruby agreed.

At that moment they heard voices near the balloons. Anton slipped behind the shed while Ruby continued butting the basket with her snout. The voices sounded like two men arguing.

"I still don't see why we don't just take them out by horse-cart, boss," said one of the men, his voice sounding young and agitated to Anton's ears. "It'd be a lot easier than flying them away like we've—"

The other man's voice, older and ill-tempered, cut him off. "Zip it, Roscoe! I've already explained this. The security at the main gates is monstrous. Those guards check every bag and box for contraband—we'd be caught in a red-hot minute! On top of that there's a detective on this case, snooping around with a bloodhound, no less. That's the last thing we need! This way, we go in the air, nobody sees a thing."

Anton peeked carefully around the corner and stifled a gasp. One of the men was wearing a green cap! The pair of them stood a short distance away from the yellow balloon, but they hadn't yet noticed the dog in the shadow of the shed. Ruby lifted the basket by the strap with her teeth and dropped it in the grass, but the latch still held. Anton was glad Ruby was still trying to get it open, though he wondered why all the jostling hadn't woken Cecil up by now.

"Psst," he whispered to Ruby. "We have to get Cecil out of here. That man has a green cap, and they might come over this way."

Ruby eyed the men and nodded. "I'll just retrieve one piece of evidence that I found inside, and then we'll hightail it. We can drag the basket home to Mr. Morgan. He can get it open for us, I'm sure." She trotted around the corner and slipped into the shed. Anton watched the two men, wishing they would leave. He knew they had something to do with the missing dogs, but he was more worried about Cecil at the moment.

"Now quit asking questions and do your job, all right?" said the green cap man.

"Yes sir, absolutely sir," said the younger man, pulling a bright yellow scarf out of his pocket and tying it around his neck. "How many are making the trip today?"

Anton jumped at the sight of the scarf. These two must be the thieves, for sure!

"Only the one you got yesterday," said the green cap man irritably. "Should have been two, but the other one bit me and got away this morning. Ungrateful mutt."

The young man whistled. "No circus for him."

"And no payday for us," growled the older man. "The basket's behind the shed. Get it and load it, will you? I'll give my regards to the crowd." He took a few steps away and then turned back, wagging a finger. "And do it right this time. No mistakes!"

"You can count on me, sir," said the younger man as his boss disappeared around the towering balloon. He turned and hurried toward the shed, pausing briefly by the door.

Anton pressed himself into the shadows next to the shed. *Maybe the balloons are lifting off. Maybe the men will get in them and leave, and we can take a good look around this place.* He heard a slam and saw the man jogging around to the back wall. The crowd of people on the wood planks began to cheer wildly at whatever the green cap man was saying to them. Under the screams and cheers, he thought he could hear a dog barking, an angry, anxious baying. But his attention was diverted by what happened next.

The yellow scarf man stepped to the basket where it lay on its side in the grass, scooped it up by its strap, and shouldered it with a groan. Anton's mouth fell open. The man was taking the basket, with Cecil inside!

"Cecil!" Anton screeched and leaped from his hiding place. "Ruby!" But Ruby didn't appear and the man was moving swiftly away, headed for the balloons. Anton raced after him. Where was he going with Cecil? And where was Ruby? Anton glanced over his shoulder and spotted the closed shed door at the same instant he recognized that the barking was coming from inside. *Oh, my whiskers!* Ruby was trapped!

There was no time to go back. Anton sprinted toward the yellow scarf man, catching up just as he reached the green balloon. He swung open the door of the gondola, dropped the basket into one corner, and was just stepping out again when Anton ran headfirst into the man's boots.

"Hey, watch it!" cried the man, shoving Anton aside. "Get outta here, cat." He clicked the gondola door shut and strode off toward the yellow balloon, past the stands where the green hat man squawked loudly to the crowd through a wide tube held up to his mouth. Two other men began adjusting the ropes that ran from the balloons to several stakes in the ground. They unlooped the ropes from two of the stakes, and the balloons bobbed a few feet up and settled back down, like ships drifting away from the docks toward the open sea.

The balloon was leaving, with Cecil aboard! Anton dashed from side to side searching for another way in, then circled the whole gondola, avoiding the ropes and stakes, calling to his brother.

"Cecil! Can you hear me? You've got to get out of there!" But Anton heard nothing from the basket. He backed up and looked at the gondola. The sides sloped outward as they rose and would be

awkward to climb, but Anton had no better option. He ran hard at one side and leaped up, hooking onto the rough wooden slats with his claws. He hung for a second, adjusting his balance on his back legs. The crowd roared again and he leaned out to see the green cap man give a big wave and turn purposefully toward the green balloon—the very one Anton was clinging to. Anton pushed off his legs and surged up a foot or more, reattaching his claws. It was working, but he was running out of time. He scooted up a few more inches.

The green cap man arrived at the gondola and stepped inside, standing at the railing right next to where Cecil's basket lay on the floor.

"Ready, Roscoe?" he yelled across to the yellow scarf man in the yellow balloon, who returned a jaunty salute. "Ready, boys?" he called to the workers poised by the stakes in the ground that held each balloon. "On three! . . . One . . . two . . ."

"Just a second, boss," called one worker close behind Anton. He stepped over and swatted Anton off the side of the gondola and into the grass, where he landed on his feet. "Almost had a stowaway there. All clear!"

Anton scrambled to make another run at the

gondola, but at that moment he heard the green cap man shout, "Three!" The workers yanked the stakes from the ground and the two balloons launched simultaneously into the air amid raucous cheering and hollering from the crowd. Anton ran underneath and jumped as high as he could, but there was nothing left to grab on to—the balloons rose above the ground with a great whooshing sound, the ropes trailing and twirling. The men in the balloons each leaned over the edge of their gondola and waved to the crowd.

Anton's throat tightened and he looked wildly around. *What can I do?* he thought desperately. He raced back to the shed and called through the space around the door.

"Ruby! They put Cecil in the balloon and flew away with him!" Anton had a few seconds to think about how bad that situation sounded before he heard Ruby's reply.

"I'll be right with you, Anton!" she cried from inside, near the back wall.

Anton skittered around the corner in time to hear a crunching *thud*: Ruby was storming her way out. A wide, splintering board protruded a few inches from the shed wall, and with another shove the nails creaked, the wood plank cracked, and the big dog barreled out into the field. She and Anton galloped to where the balloons had been a minute before and gazed up.

"Oh, no," cried Ruby. "This can't be."

The humans in the stands peered into the sky, shading their eyes from the sun and shouting. "Go, Lion, win it!" "Onward, Tiger, you can beat him!" Some spilled onto the field and jumped up and down, waving their arms at the balloonists. Ruby and Anton watched the balloons go, the two shapes stark against the clouds, gradually diminishing as they rose.

Anton's heart beat crazily and he found it hard to breathe. "Ruby," he said in a strangled gasp. "How will I . . ."

Ruby leaned and touched her wet black nose to the top of Anton's head. "Find Cecil. Yes, I know, my dear. We'll figure something out, don't you worry. I'm quite good at this sort of thing."

But Anton knew what Ruby wasn't saying. "You can't track him now, can you?"

"Not this way, I'm afraid. Not through the air." She shook her head briskly and huffed. "But they'll be back. Those scoundrels run these balloons every day, and when they come back, we'll see what we can see. Or, rather, smell."

Anton nodded weakly. Maybe Cecil would come back, too. He would have to hope.

Ruby glanced once more at the balloons, now small in the distance, and tipped her head toward Anton. "In the meantime, come with me. There may be someone we *can* rescue, right this minute."

CHAPTER 8

Cecil Aloft

A great chuffing sound awoke Cecil. He blinked blearily, trying to remember where he was. It was dark and chilly, and he felt oddly light-headed. As he got to his paws he realized he was confined in a small space—some kind of box or basket, he guessed, given the tiny bands of light filtering in. He rose up on his back legs and bumped his head against the top to push it open, but it didn't budge. Then he began to remember. The field near the balloons with Anton and Ruby. The shed, the baskets, the sleepiness.

I must still be in the basket, Cecil thought. *Why*

can't I get out? And where is Anton now? He pressed his face against the wicker slats and peered out. He could see a very small room with a few boxes and bags and one pair of human legs in it. *Who's this?* He couldn't see the top of the human, but Cecil could hear him humming to himself. It was odd that he could see shadows on the floor and felt a chill in the little room. He squirmed in the basket, trying to get a better view.

"Ah!" said the man through the slats of the container. "You're awake. Quiet, though. Not a barker or a whiner, are you? Good. How about some water before we land?" He opened a bag and brought out a bowl, which he filled with water from a bottle and set on the floor. "We'll freshen you up for the sale." The man chuckled to himself—a grating, tittering sound—as he stepped up to the basket, bumping it with the toe of his boot.

Cecil heard the man fiddling with the latch of his prison cell and readied his back legs. The basket lid cracked open a few inches and Cecil could see the man's eyes peering into the dark interior.

"Hold on a second," said the man, frowning, "you sure don't look—"

Cecil sprang upward, driving his head and

forelegs through the opening. The lid snapped from the man's hand and he yelped in surprise and stumbled back. Cecil surged out of the basket, landing on the rough planked floor, and dashed to the far side of the tiny room. There were very few places to hide, but he squeezed between two canvas bags and turned quickly to see if the man was pursuing him. The man sat where he'd fallen on the floor and stared after Cecil, his mouth hanging open.

"What in blazes . . . ?" he spluttered. The man's face turned a shade of crimson and he slapped his palm to his forehead. "You're no puppy—you're a cat! Oh, when I get my hands on that Roscoe . . . !"

Cecil crouched behind the bags as the man struggled to his feet. He took two steps and lunged for Cecil, who sprang away with a yowl. The gondola bounced and tilted as man and cat circled, and the ropes holding the balloon in place groaned with the strain. After two trips darting from corner to corner, Cecil ended up behind the bags again and the man stopped, his hands on his hips, breathing heavily. Cecil watched him talk to himself for a moment. The man was wearing a green cap, so he must be the thief they'd been looking for, but where were Anton and Ruby?

Then Cecil looked up, and his heart leaped. *A balloon!*

The gigantic green balloon towered over them in the cloudy blue sky, tilting and billowing in the wind. The gondola, which Cecil finally understood they were riding in, pitched and swung as the ropes connecting it creaked like the timbers on a ship. *I've got to see this!* he thought, abandoning all caution. He darted out from behind the bags to the top of a crate.

Clinging tightly with his claws, Cecil leaned out to take in a view more astounding than he had ever imagined. The Furs Wheel had lifted Anton and him to commanding heights, but this was much higher than that. *So this is what birds see,* Cecil thought. *I'm actually flying!* He blinked a few times to clear his dizzy head and gazed down at the wide spaces inhabited by tiny buildings and the curves of narrow blue rivers winding through the fields. Train tracks ran in dark stripes across the land, and away to the right lay a vast body of water, glinting in the sunlight, miniature ships moving slowly over the surface. *That must be the lake we saw from the Fair—it's gigantic!*

Cecil turned and saw the yellow balloon at

about the same height but far away, and he wondered briefly where it was going. The ride was so quiet—unlike the blustery, chuffing trains—that Cecil could hear the voices of people on the ground and dogs barking. Some of the people looked up at the passing balloon and waved their arms. Why did humans like to do that so often? But he had little time to enjoy the view as, just behind him, the man in the green cap began talking at him again.

"I don't know how you got into that basket, cat." The man huffed, adjusting his cap and straightening his coat. "I ought to just throw you overboard." He glowered at Cecil, who watched the man from over his shoulder. "I will, too, if need be. Don't think I won't." The man continued grumbling as he surveyed the landscape over one rail of the gondola, then shook his head. "And now we're off course, thanks to you!" He grabbed the dangling ropes attached to the great balloon, tugging on some and looping others around metal hooks sticking up from the floor.

Cecil watched from his high post as the man worked to bring the balloon under control. The man yanked hard on a slim rope dangling from inside the balloon, and Cecil heard a sharp hissing sound.

"Uh-oh," muttered the man.

As he surveyed the ground again, Cecil saw the fields and rivers below getting nearer. *Where will we land?* he thought, suddenly wondering how he would find his way back to the Fair. He glanced behind and could still spot the towering Furs Wheel in the distance. *It won't be so easy to see once we're on the ground.* He gazed ahead and gasped at a more immediate problem. The balloon was sinking rapidly, and Cecil didn't like the looks of the landing area. *Great cats in heaven. We're headed directly for the lake.*

The man was frantically throwing anything he could find, the barrel, a chair, a metal box, even the basket Cecil had come in, over the side into the lake. *I'll be next,* Cecil thought, and sure enough the man turned on him with a gleam in his eye.

"Sorry, tubby," said the man, lurching across the deeply slanted floor to where Cecil stood.

I don't think so. He leaped down from the crate and slid across the floor to the other side. The man turned his attention to the crate, which went over the side and made an audible splash. The balloon was going down fast, like a sinking ship. The man lurched to the ropes, hauling them this way and that and grasping at the stiff edge of the balloon itself. Cecil pulled himself up by the claws to look over the side of the gondola. The churning water was beckoning with white-topped waves, so close now Cecil let out a frightened yowl.

"We're going to crash," the man cried, and in the next moment, with a sound like a diving whale's tail, the gondola smacked into the water. The balloon widened and flattened overhead, descending gently like a rain cloud. Cecil dropped back onto the floor with one question burning in his brain: *Will this thing float?*

For the moment, it did, while the balloon folded over and around it. A splash of water came in one side, then the other. *We're going to be trapped in here!* Cecil thought. The man had the same idea and climbed up on one side of the gondola, but he lost his balance and fell backward into the water. The gondola tipped abruptly after him and Cecil slid across the floor, struggling to right himself and striking the wall headfirst. His claws saved him from pitching in after the man. Cecil could see the man treading furiously in the water while the heavy curtain of the balloon settled over him.

"Help!" the man cried. "Save me!"

Without thinking Cecil leaped out of the gondola and onto the strange fabric of the balloon. *This stuff floats, too,* he realized. It was forming itself into a kind of raft, with a low spot at the center that steadily filled with water. Beneath the edge where the gondola held the cloth above the water, Cecil could see the man's frantic efforts to get out from under it. He battled it with his hands, shouting all the while.

He needs to rip the balloon, Cecil thought. And his next thought sent him gingerly hopping across the rubbery surface: *This is a job for claws.* When he was close enough to feel the rise and fall of the balloon fabric stretched over the gasping captive, Cecil crouched low and popped out all his claws. Then he began the pleasurable business of tearing and tearing with all his strength, while trying very hard not to get his fur wet.

The material was stiff but it had a fine weave to it, and after only a few tries he'd produced a hole big enough to catch in his claws and pull wider. The man had stopped thrashing and seemed to know what Cecil was doing. As the weave gave and a nice tear opened wide, the man's hand came through and gripped the edge. Cecil avoided catching the hand with his claws as he pulled harder and harder. Another hand appeared and then Cecil's claws found a thin strip and a very satisfying rip opened a hole big enough for the man's head and shoulder to come through. Cecil leaped away from the hole, and the man stared at Cecil in amazement.

"You saved my life," he said, pulling himself up onto the still-floating balloon. "I can't believe it. A cat saved my life."

Cecil was thinking about his own life now, as the balloon was steadily taking on water. The gondola rested half on and half off the balloon, which served to keep it afloat. But it wouldn't last long, Cecil observed, and once it was filled with water it would sink, pulling the balloon fabric down with it. He watched as the man stumbled toward it, groaning and pulling at the fur on his face.

There's no sense in that, Cecil thought. He pulled himself up to the highest point of the sinking balloon—it was like trying to climb a bubble.

All around the water was churning, and Cecil recalled how big the lake had looked from the sky. He swiveled his ears front to back—there was a sound he hadn't noticed before, a chugging, humming rumble getting closer every moment. He stretched his neck up and gazed over the water and it seemed to him that he saw a white object, like a pipe, and a white cloud as well billowing into the blue sky overhead. Then he heard a human voice cry out and another voice he didn't recognize but understood.

It was a cat. "We're coming!" she called. "We're coming to get you."

The ship sent out a deafening blare, like a goose honking inside Cecil's head. At this the man shouted joyfully and rushed back from the gondola, which made a sucking sound as it slipped a little deeper into the water.

"Calm down," Cecil called to him, but of course the man had no idea what he was saying. He shouted something and applied himself to crawling on all fours toward the high vista Cecil occupied, pulling the balloon down as he clambered up. Cecil could see the prow of the ship now. It was small, without sails, full of humans on two decks and cutting fast through the waves.

Again the feline on the deck called out, "Hang on! We'll be there soon."

All we can do *is hang on,* thought Cecil, shaking his wet paws one by one.

When the ship was closer, all the humans and the man began shouting, and two sailors threw down a heavy white ring with ropes attached to it. The man leaped into the water, grasped the edge and lifted it over his head, which then came up inside the ring. He was floating nicely and the sailors began hauling him in with the rope.

Cecil watched the man, blubbering and howling, being pulled up onto the deck, throwing his arms around the Captain who quickly passed him to a sailor, and then going off into the throng without so much as a look back at Cecil.

"Hey, what about me?" Cecil shouted. Now he could see the cat on the deck, a small orange female with a white streak down her nose.

"You've got to get hold of a ring," she shouted back.

"Can you get them to throw one out to me?"

The orange cat commenced yowling loudly and pacing on the deck in great agitation, attracting the attention of the passengers. A lady standing at the rail spotted Cecil and said something to her neighbor, who repeated it, and it was passed on until a throng of excited humans was shouting, "THE CAT, THE CAT!"

Splat, another ring hit the water very near Cecil's solitary and sinking post, and he eyed it dubiously. *If it can float a man, it can float a cat,* Cecil reasoned. He hesitated a few more seconds, trying to think of a way to grab the ring without getting completely drenched, but it was no use. Hoping only that he would be able to get some purchase on the surface, he leaped for it, landing with his front legs gripping the inside of the ring and his back legs hanging over the outside, dipping in and out of the cold, choppy lake. It was rough and even a little stretchy—his claws held him in place, and the sailors, to the delight of the human audience, began hauling him toward the ship.

❖ ❖ ❖

The sailor who pulled Cecil in wrapped him in a cloth and rubbed him down before setting him on very wobbly legs on the deck. By now, the humans had gotten over the excitement of the rescue and drifted away from the rails, and the orange cat who had called from the ship ran to Cecil.

"I cannot believe you were on that balloon!" she exclaimed. "We all saw it go down. How on earth did you manage to hitch a ride on that monster?"

Cecil was giving his ears a last going over and smoothing the fur on his shoulder. "Believe me," he said to the strange, bold little cat, "it wasn't my choice."

"I'm Kitty," she said. "Though the humans call me Cleopatra. But it's actually just Kitty."

"My name is Cecil. Do you live on this ship?"

"I've been here since I was a kitten. The Captain brought me on and I have the run of the place. We ferry people and animals from one shore to the other, back and forth. I've seen ships that are bigger and have sails, and whose cats tell me they go much farther."

"I've been on one of those," Cecil declared. "I've sailed to warm islands and seen exotic places, strange animals. I was even captured by pirates."

"Pirates!" Kitty exclaimed. "That sounds exciting."

"They're not very nice, actually."

"So you've been to sea and now you've been in a balloon!"

Cecil couldn't resist the chance to impress his

new friend. "And I've been to the land of the set-ting sun in a train."

"Rolling death?" She shuddered. "There's a sta-tion for one of those near the dock on the other side." She looked over her shoulder through the rail at the wide water. "Some of the ferry passen-gers cross the wharf to a big station and then they get on the train. A dog who passed through here told me the trains go to the sea, the one where the sun rises, and that there are more ships there that go all over the world."

The sea where the sun rises! "That's where I'm from and that's where I'm bound," Cecil said. "As soon as I catch up with my brother. Thank you for telling mc how to get there."

"Is your brother in the other balloon? I see it every so often. We're heading for the place where it's supposed to land."

Anton! Cecil thought. *And Ruby! Even Ruby couldn't track a balloon. How will they find me?*

"We're on a case," Cecil told Kitty. "We're track-ing a couple of men who steal puppies. One of them was the fellow on the balloon with me. What hap-pened to him?"

"My Captain took him to his quarters. He is a very upset human. I've never seen one carry on like that."

"He's a thief and a coward," Cecil said gloomily. "I saved his life and he left me to drown."

The ferry was cutting swiftly through the water and a few humans came from the inner rooms to look out over the lake. "We're getting close to the landing," Kitty said. "Look. You can see the tent from here."

Cecil looked out over the lake. He could make out the shoreline and above it, over the crest of a hill and beyond a grove of trees, a few scattered buildings and the white top of a huge tent. "What's in the tent?" he asked.

"They call it a circus," Kitty said. "I've heard they have some unusual animals there. They put on shows and humans go there to see them."

"Sounds a bit like the Fair, where I just came from," Cecil said. "That's where my man is going, I'll wager."

More and more humans came out on the deck, talking and laughing. A great many children approached the cats with outstretched hands. "Come with me," Kitty said, skirting the crowd. "We can wait outside the Captain's quarters and when the man comes out you can follow him."

Cecil bustled along behind the young cat. He wished he had more time to talk with her. But for now his mission was to follow the very bad man who had nearly let him drown.

"Good plan," he said to Kitty. "Maybe once we catch our man, we'll come back this way."

Kitty looked over her shoulder and Cecil heard her purr. "I'd like that very much," she said.

CHAPTER 9

Cat Trackers

Who?" asked Anton miserably, in no mood for games after watching his brother fly away, trapped in an immense green balloon. "*Who* can we rescue?"

"Come on, follow me," said Ruby. The throng of humans milled on the field and gazed at the two balloons in the distance, still shouting and cheering. "I may very well be wrong, but then again I might be right. And if I'm right, and I do hope that I am, then we need to move quickly." She trotted away, her nose to the ground as usual. With one last glance at the faraway balloon, Anton scampered after her, his heart squeezing in his chest.

Ruby led them back around the shed, straight to the lone basket leaning against the wall near one corner. She inhaled deeply, and Anton drew close and sniffed as well.

"There's so much puppy smell around here that I almost missed this," said Ruby. "It was only when your brother was taken that I thought of it, to be honest."

"Missed what?" asked Anton, distracted with thoughts of Cecil aloft, high above the city.

Ruby lowered her nose again and nudged the basket gently onto its side. It thumped in the grass as if it contained some weight, and a small, muffled whimper arose from inside.

Anton stiffened, his ears pricked forward. "What's that?" he cried. "Who's in there?"

"Well," said Ruby, pawing at the latch, "I'm hoping it's the someone we can rescue." The latch held, just as the one on Cecil's basket had, and she snorted in frustration. "You see, it occurred to me that if those men are the dognappers, and they didn't know that *Cecil* was inside that basket, they must have assumed they were taking a puppy with them in the balloon."

Anton's eyes opened wide. "You think they picked up the wrong basket?"

"That's what I think. And that means . . ."

"They left a dog behind," finished Anton, circling around the basket on the ground.

Ruby nodded. "You've got it. But there's only one way to be sure. We have to get a human to open this for us. And there's only one that I trust." She grasped the long leather strap with her teeth and stretched it out along the grass. "Can you hold this up for me?"

Anton stepped to the strap and clenched it in his jaws, lifting his chin to raise it as high as he could. Ruby slid her head underneath and then stood up, hoisting the basket so it hung across her shoulders like a bulky necklace.

"You look like a fisher-dog," said Anton, impressed with Ruby's strength.

"Let's see if we can make it to Mr. Morgan's house without arousing suspicion." Another groggy moan came from the basket. "Shhh, little one," Ruby said, looking down. "We'll get you out of there. Just hold tight."

Voices from the field carried over as humans wandered near the shed. Anton and Ruby exchanged a nod, and Anton turned and led the way toward Morgan's street. Ruby followed, as stealthy as a big dog with a burden could be.

⚜ ⚜ ⚜

It took quite a while for the pair to navigate the crowds. They slipped behind buildings when they could, and Ruby moved slowly to avoid bouncing the basket too much against her legs. The humans who did catch sight of them stopped and pointed, as if the spectacle of Anton and Ruby marching along were just another curious part of the Fair. It was well after midday as they rounded the corner of the street where Morgan lived, and right away they noticed activity out front.

Two ladies dressed in long, frilly frocks and elaborate hats, one with yellow hair and sharp blue eyes and the other gray and stooped, sat on the porch with Morgan. The younger lady spoke rapidly in a shrill voice, gesturing widely with her arms, while the older lady clasped her hands together and shook her head slowly, her face mournful. Mr. Morgan leaned toward them in his chair, nodding and writing on a pad of paper in his lap. Anton and

Ruby stopped at the bottom of the porch steps and gazed up at the group. Ruby sat down, resting the basket's weight on the ground in front of her paws.

"And now we don't know where to turn, you understand, Mr. Morgan?" the younger lady exclaimed. "Alexandrine is a very valuable dog, a purebred Italian spitz, and my goodness, who could have done such a thing?" She began to weep pitifully, and Morgan reached out and offered her a handkerchief from his pocket.

The older lady clutched a length of rope in her hand, and Anton saw that it was a leash, cut straight across on one end. *Another victim,* Anton thought, and he glanced up at Ruby with wide eyes. Ruby must have noticed the same thing, as she gave a soft *woof* to get Morgan's attention. He looked over at Ruby in surprise.

"Not now, LeNez," he said, waving his hand and frowning slightly. "I'm busy here."

The younger lady accepted the handkerchief and blew her nose loudly, while the older lady gazed down at the bloodhound.

"What a beautiful dog you have, Mr. Morgan," she said.

"Thank you," said Morgan, "though she's a bit rude today. I do apologize."

Ruby stood up and took a step forward. *Woof, woof,* she tried again.

"I do believe she's trying to tell you something," the older lady observed.

"Always a distinct possibility with LeNez. Excuse me for a moment, would you?" Morgan set his pen and pad down and stepped off the porch.

Ruby bent her head forward and slipped out of the strap across her shoulders, then stood waiting by the basket.

"Now what is it, LeNez?" asked Morgan, stopping in front of the big dog. "Where did you find this fishing basket?"

"I wish he'd just open it, for goodness' sake," she murmured to Anton.

Anton circled the basket, mewing and dragging his tail along the latch to highlight the point. From the basket came a small whine. Morgan froze, his eyebrows arched. On the porch, the younger woman straightened and turned sharply in her chair.

Morgan knelt and unhooked the cord from the latch. Slowly he raised the lid and peeked inside.

"Oh, good heavens, LeNez," he exclaimed softly. "What have you brought to us?" He reached in and gently lifted out a shivering white dog. As he turned toward the porch, cradling the puppy in his arms, the two ladies rose from their chairs, staring. All three humans stood for a moment with their mouths agape.

"Alexandrine!" said the younger woman, her voice quavering. "Our puppy! You found her!"

The humans turned in unison to stare at Ruby in awe and wonder.

Ruby winked at Anton and wagged her tail.

⚘ ⚘ ⚘

"Perhaps now we'll finally get some help on this case," said Ruby late in the afternoon as her partner and the other detectives carefully searched the grassy field for clues. After the reunion of the puppy with the overjoyed owners, Ruby had led her intrigued partner back to the balloon field. Morgan had snooped around the empty field and the shed, and had called in other detectives from the Fair to help.

"I wouldn't bet on it," said Anton glumly. He sat with his tail curled around his front paws, his eyes fixed on the sky, where the green balloon that had taken Cecil away was notably absent. "They're gone, Ruby. Who knows where?"

In addition to feeling helpless and worried sick,

Anton was furious with himself. He watched miserably, thinking over and over about the way Cecil had been separated from him, and he chastised himself for not preventing it. "I should never have let him get in that basket," said Anton fiercely as the detectives crisscrossed the field like scurrying mice.

Ruby gazed down at the small gray cat. "I doubt you could have stopped him, Anton, even if you knew what was going to happen. Keep your chin up, my friend. All we need is one small clue now. I'm positive that something will present itself very shortly. We just need to stay alert!"

Anton nodded and the two of them began their own search of the field. Ruby trailed after Morgan and the other detectives in case they found anything useful in places she couldn't see or reach. Anton sniffed the trampled grass where the gondolas had rested, traced the trail of footprints leading to and from the area, and scoured the interior of the ramshackle shed—at least until a policeman chased him out. But though Anton remained as alert as he could, he found no hint as to Cecil's whereabouts, and his heart drummed heavily in his chest. The terrible thought of life without his brother began to creep into his mind, and he quickly shoved it away.

When the sun had dipped below the horizon and the work of the investigators had stalled, Ruby and Anton rested under a nearby tent awning and compared notes. Ruby had sniffed out a dog collar in the weeds of the field, which she had presented to Morgan. Inside the shed, Anton dragged a musty piece of fabric from under a box in the corner, remembering Cecil's comment about some strange-smelling "damp cloth." This cloth was dry, but crinkly like it had been wet once, and after some exertions Anton was able to get the detectives to take notice of it on the floor. They sniffed the cloth and nodded to each other.

"Chloroform," one said, tucking it away in a bag. "Somebody's up to no good."

"How's about the two of us go and find something to eat?" Ruby suggested when they had found no more clues for some time. "Then we'll come back and make another pass."

Anton hesitated. "What if Cecil comes back, and we're not here?"

"He's smart enough to think of going to Mr. Morgan's house, where we'd find him soon enough," said Ruby.

"You're right, he is," said Anton. "But let's make it quick, anyway."

Just as the dog and cat were about to leave the field, Anton looked up to see a horse approaching, pulling a cart with a young man sitting in the driver's seat up top.

"Ruby!" cried Anton, craning his neck to track the man on the cart. "The driver!"

Ruby whirled and squinted, following Anton's gaze. "Ah! It may be our lucky break. That's one of the men who flew off in the balloons, isn't that right?"

"Yes! Do you see Cecil?" Anton dashed from side to side, trying to catch a glimpse into the cart from where they stood.

"No, not from here," said Ruby. "But the cart is filled with things, so he may very well be tucked in there somewhere."

As soon as the detectives noticed the cart, the scene turned chaotic. Morgan and the others hustled over and everyone began talking at once. The detectives gestured toward the field and the shed, speaking tersely. The balloonist, wearing a yellow scarf around his neck, stepped down from the cart shaking his head, his hands held out wide.

Ruby put her big front paws up in the cart, sniffing for Cecil, but a detective shooed her away. She and Anton circled the cart, calling Cecil's name.

"He could be still sleeping," suggested Anton hopefully.

"Maybe," said Ruby, "but I'm not smelling him here, I'm afraid."

They looked back at the man in the center of the group of detectives. Morgan held up the cut leash and pointed at him, but he shrugged and said nothing.

"That's the one from the other balloon," said Anton. "But I'll bet he knows where my brother is. If only I could make him tell me!" Before he could stop himself, Anton darted between the detectives right up to the man and stood on his back legs. He clutched the man's trousers with his claws, staring into his eyes. "Where is Cecil?" he hissed.

The man yelped and shook his leg to dislodge Anton. One of the detectives stepped forward and grasped Anton by the back of his neck, pulling him off and holding him up in the air. The yellow scarf man stared at the gray cat, wide-eyed, then turned away as the detective tossed Anton down in the grass near Ruby.

"We're not going to get anything out of this fellow," said Ruby grimly. "Though if I know Mr. Morgan, he'll keep trying for quite a while."

"Don't they know that this is one of the crimi-nals?" Anton said with a huff. "Isn't it obvious?"

Ruby sighed. "Perhaps they can't be sure—not if there are no puppies in evidence."

Anton turned to Ruby, scowling. "We can't wait for these humans to talk all day! *Why* isn't Cecil here?" He gazed up to the empty sky again. When he turned back to Ruby, she wasn't there. "Ruby?"

"Over here," Ruby called softly from near the horse-cart. As Anton approached, Ruby stepped directly in front of the blinkered horse. "Hello, there," she called up.

"Whoa, there, dog!" whinnied the horse, shift-ing on his hooves. "Don't stand so close!"

"I'm sorry," said Ruby. "But I wondered if I might ask you a question."

"A question? Well. All right, I suppose, but I'm quite busy, as you can see." The horse drew him-self up and shook his bridle but continued to stand on the packed dirt of the Midway, doing not much of anything.

Ruby exchanged glances with Anton and nod-ded. "Yes, of course, I'll get right to the point. Can you tell us where you have come from, just now?"

"Tell us?" said the horse, blinking. "Who is *us*?"

"My name is Ruby, and this is Anton," said Ruby, tilting her head toward the gray cat.

The horse turned his head so the narrow view of his blinkers suddenly included Anton. "Oh my! A cat! First a dog, and now a cat, too. This is really too much." He licked his lips nervously.

"Are you all right?" Ruby inquired.

"Well I think I will be, if there aren't any more of you," said the horse.

"No, there are just the two of us."

"Good," said the horse. "I'm Sedgwick. I'm a Thoroughbred, you know. A race horse. Retired now, but still in top form. And I don't usually chat with strangers."

"Of course you don't," said Ruby. "We'll be gone in a twinkling. Now, to my question, if you would be so kind. Where have you just come from?"

The horse sighed and commenced thinking, his eyes rolling around in between the confines of the blinkers. "Before coming here, I was at the circus," he announced.

"The circus!" exclaimed Ruby. "Ah ha, we're making progress. And can you tell me how I would get there? Or rather, how you got here from there?"

The horse looked dubiously down his long nose

at Ruby. "Well that's another question, isn't it? Two more, really."

"It is. Can you tell me?"

"It's really important!" cried Anton, unable to contain his impatience. The horse shied away from the little cat.

"All right, all right!" said the horse. "No need to yell. Let me think." He thought again, his tongue sticking out between his teeth. Finally he shook his head. "No. I can't tell you."

Ruby opened her mouth but Anton jumped in. "What do you mean, 'no'? Tell us!"

"I mean, I have no idea how I got here!" neighed the horse, his nostrils puffing. "Furthermore, I simply don't care. The driver pulls the reins, I turn the way he pulls, and I watch the road as we go. It's the same on a racetrack. I don't look about at landmarks, you understand? My job is speed and efficiency, not directions."

Anton glared at the horse. "But, surely . . ."

The horse turned his head so he couldn't see Anton. "My name is Sedgwick. Don't call me Shirley. Now that's quite enough questioning for one day."

"But—"

"Anton, I have another idea," Ruby interrupted, motioning him over to the big wheel on one side of the cart.

"Do you know what's this 'circus' he's talking about?" asked Anton, following the bloodhound. "That could be where they left Cecil."

Ruby squinted. "I have a vague idea, only from talking to an animal or two that has escaped from it." Anton's eyes widened, but Ruby focused on the cart wheel, sniffing around the entire circumference.

"How can that silly horse not know where he just came from?" said Anton with disgust.

Ruby turned to him, her eyes bright. "That may not matter, my friend."

"Why not?" asked Anton.

"I think I may be able to track this cart backwards to there from here. The wheels smell strongly of certain exotic animals, sawdust, and sweet, sticky food. Different enough from the Fair scents that I should be able to backtrack, at least for a while, depending on how far it is. It will be dark soon—we'd have to wait until morning to set out." Ruby cocked her head at Anton. "What do you say? Shall we give it a try?"

Anton stared at Ruby. The thought of leaving the Fair altogether made him dizzy with worry, but they had to follow this clue while they had it. He gazed across to the yellow scarf man, still surrounded by a cluster of detectives in the field. He was of no use now that Cecil was somewhere else.

Anton drew himself up and nodded grimly. "I say, let's get ourselves to the circus."

CHAPTER 10

Under the Big Top

ecil meowed a quick thanks and goodbye to Kitty on the ferry before trotting down the gangplank in pursuit of the balloon man. The man had lost his green cap in the lake and had traded his sodden Fair clothes for the gray shirt and trousers the ferry crew wore, so he was difficult to pick out in the crowd. Cecil zigged and zagged behind the man, who strode rapidly past the other humans on the landing and made his way up a wide, tree-lined avenue.

If I can just keep up with him, Cecil thought, *he'll*

lead me straight to the puppies. After that, the thorny problem of how to find his way back to the Fair, and his brother and Ruby, would have to be solved.

The sun hung in the sky above the avenue like the lantern of an oncoming train, and Cecil squinted into the glare, trying to hold the man in his sights. A sudden shout to one side caught his attention, and he slowed to watch a strange human with a woman's voice, smiling and calling out to the people strolling by. The human had skin as pale as the snow on the Ice Railway, a wide, steeply curved red mouth, and mounds of red curls protruding from under a pointed hat. Her clothes shimmered and billowed, covered with small spots of many different colors, and she waved and chattered to all who passed her. Her feet were enclosed in huge black shoes, but most curious to Cecil was the bundle of thin cords she held in one hand, each attached to a bobbing balloon. The balloons were shaped like the one that had carried him here, but were only the size of a human's head. The odd-looking lady was handing the miniature balloons on strings to the children in the crowd, and directing everyone up the avenue with a fat gloved finger.

"Mommy, a clown, a clown!" cried one young girl, pointing eagerly.

"A clown!" shouted another child, pulling his father's hand. "Can we go see?"

Cecil used Ruby's trick to divine that this character was apparently named "Aclown," and marveled for another moment before remembering the green cap man. With a jolt he peered forward again, but his heart was already sinking. *Cat's whiskers!* He'd lost the man.

Now what? Cecil turned in a slow circle. Kitty had said that the balloonists often landed near the circus, so the man might be headed that way. He looked again at Aclown, who continued to prattle and wave, gesturing up the avenue. Kitty had also said that humans went to the circus in crowds. Maybe Aclown was part of it, showing the way.

Keeping close to the buildings on one side to avoid being trampled, Cecil hurried along until the road rose slightly. Cresting the rise, he blinked as the sun sank below the city skyline. Straight ahead, framed in the red-orange light, Cecil saw the pointed white spires of a huge tent. A small bit of hope flared in Cecil's chest and he picked up his pace. He might still be able to catch up with the green cap man. *Leave me to drown, but you can't shake me, you thieving hoodlum. Cecil is on the case.*

✣ ✣ ✣

Jangly music and salty, fatty smells floated to Cecil as he drew near the grassy area surrounding the big tent in the twilight of the day. He crept along the perimeter, cautious and alert, his tail twitching. Humans inside the tent clapped and laughed at whatever it was they were watching, and shadows flickered on the white canvas, ripped in a few places so that the lantern light spilled out. Cecil rounded a corner and an entirely different set of smells filled his nose—the musk and bedding of caged animals. The field was edged by a stretch of weedy track upon which stood a line of battered train carriages with open, barred sides, some of them empty but others containing creatures Cecil could not immediately identify. He stared, his ears swiveling to listen to the chatter.

"When are they going to feed us?" called one deep voice to a neighboring carriage. "I'm hungry."

"Soon, I hope," replied a second voice. "Though I don't look forward to that wilted lettuce."

"Stifling hot today, wasn't it?" squeaked a third, high-pitched and warbling.

"And humid, yes," answered a fourth in a soft hiss. "Plus, I seem to be sharing my cage with a whole host of spiders."

Kitty said the animals perform in shows for the humans, thought Cecil. *I wonder what they do in there?* He peered up at the giant tent. The pointed spires at the top were lopsided, the canvas worn and frayed at the edges. From inside, the raucous music twanged with off-notes. Cecil turned and spotted a large pile of garbage behind a cluster of smaller tents, beside which a few hunched humans milled about. He imagined the puppies, confused and frightened, stashed here somewhere.

As he gazed across the field in the dusky evening air, Cecil noticed a movement in the carriage nearest to him, the last on the track. Something inside was pacing sinuously back and forth from end to end in the confined space. The creature was huge, yet lithe, never pausing, its paws making no sound at all on the floor of the cage. None of the others spoke to it, nor it to them.

Cecil took a few steps into the field, angling around to get a better look at the shadowy animal. He stifled a gasp—it was a massive *cat*, as big as a small horse but not horse-like in its shape. The cat's muscled shoulders rolled as it stalked, its wide, round head held low as if tracking prey. Anton and Cecil had encountered the Great Cat, an enormous feline, in the mountains on their train trip into the setting sun, but this one was even bigger. Cecil ventured a little closer, gawking. Like the Great Cat, this big cat had curiously curved ears, he noticed, but instead of a golden brown coat, this one was covered in bright jagged stripes that seemed to ripple as it moved. Cecil was entranced.

Very slowly, the huge cat's head began to rise as it paced. Its muzzle alone was bigger than Cecil's whole head, and it sniffed the air delicately. Finally it stopped moving and turned to Cecil, its eyes glowing in the last light of the day, unblinking. Cecil froze, all of his fur standing on end, his mouth hanging open. He couldn't speak a word, could not look away from the black-rimmed, golden eyes. The creature's wide, pink tongue appeared and swiped swiftly across its mouth.

At that moment, a sharp voice piped up close behind Cecil.

"Ah, might I have a word?" said the voice.

Cecil jumped and broke eye contact with the

huge cat. A skinny animal about his size crouched nearby, beckoning him away. He felt a small paw on his back leg, pulling.

"How about you come away from there *right now*?" implored the slight animal. "Come with me, friend, and stay alive."

Cecil allowed himself to be tugged backward as he glanced once more at the carriage. The big cat stood watching him from the shadows, its tail curling and uncurling. A wiry arm slipped across Cecil's shoulders and guided him back around the corner, out of view of the train cars. In the lamp-light leaking from inside the tent, Cecil finally sat down and took a good look at his companion.

Standing on two legs before him was a wisp of a figure covered in brown and black fur, with large side ears and close-set round eyes. Its head was round, too, and at the ends of its long arms were elongated paws that ended in leathery, almost human fingers. The whole creature resembled a tiny, furry human, except for its wiry, flicking tail.

The figure extended a paw toward Cecil. "Happy to meet you," he said, grinning. "I am Sergio, humble spider monkey originally from Costa Rica, now serving as official ambassador of the circus. I welcome you!" He grasped Cecil's paw and bowed deeply.

Cecil stared in wonder, trying to remember his manners. "Um, I'm Cecil, a common alley cat from a land far away, and I'm currently lost." He looked down at Sergio's paw clasped around his. "You have hands!"

"That I do," said Sergio, wiggling his fingers in the air. "And they come in pretty *handy*, I can assure you." He glanced behind him and lowered his voice. "Now, Cecil, I must caution you about the tiger back there."

"That huge, striped cat, you mean?" Cecil shivered. "What a creature!"

Sergio nodded gravely. "Tasha—that's her name. She is a Siberian tigress. Do not mess with her, Cecil." He wagged one long finger in front of the cat's nose. "She has a very bad temper, and it can be hazardous to your health. I have seen some approach the cage right up to the bars, drawn in by her eyes." He winced, pointing to his own eyes with two fingers. "It's not safe! So stay back, all right? Are we agreed?"

"Agreed," said Cecil, a little reluctantly. He'd

felt a wild spirit in the tigress, a raw energy that he wanted to know more about. But there were other things to do first. "I'm actually here looking for a bunch of puppies—little white dogs—that were stolen from the Fair. Have you seen any like that?"

Sergio folded his skinny arms and squinted at Cecil. "Little white dogs. Well, we have several of those who do an act in the show, of course. The dancing dogs. *Stolen* dogs—now that is a very different thing entirely." He frowned, stroking the hair on his chin. "Business is not good, but I do not believe the owners of the circus would go as far as stealing."

Cecil blinked at the monkey. Maybe Sergio knew that the puppies were stolen or maybe he didn't. Better to be careful. "Well, I'd like to meet them if you could point me in the right direction," he said carefully. "I'm a big fan of dogs," he added, putting on a goofy grin, as a cat who admired dogs would surely wear.

Sergio turned and pointed to the group of smaller tents bunched together like a tiny town in the field beyond the train carriages. "They are taught to dance in the smallest tent, in the back by the large tree." He whirled and clasped his paw-hands together. "And now, Cecil, I really must go. I am assistant master of ceremonies for the show and have many duties to perform inside." He jerked a stubby thumb toward the main tent beside them.

"I thought you were the ambassador," said Cecil.

"That too! There aren't enough humans, so I wear many hats!" The monkey scampered away, calling over his shoulder as he went. "Enjoy yourself. And keep away from the tigress!"

✤ ✤ ✤

Charting a path as far as possible from the tigress's cage, Cecil trotted over to the little tent city. He could feel Tasha's luminous eyes on him, but he dared not look her way. Humans wearing bright, tight-fitting clothes moved between the tents carrying loads of equipment, eating food from paper wrappers, and smearing their faces with colorful paints. Cecil ducked between and around them until he arrived at the last, smallest tent. He stood to one side and peered in through the open flap.

Sure enough, there were six small white dogs inside, and Cecil could hear the voices of two men shouting at each other. Cecil didn't know what types the dogs were, and they all looked slightly different from one another, but they were similar enough to Camille to give him hope. He backed up and crouched in the shadows, outside the reach of the lantern light, wondering if he was in the right place.

Suddenly, one of the men yelled something and stormed out of the tent. Cecil caught a glimpse of his face as he rushed by—it was the green cap man! *So these* must *be the stolen puppies,* he thought. Now his mission changed from tracking to rescue, and he pondered his options. It would be tricky to get past the human, for starters. And the dogs were enclosed in a mesh cage of some kind, with no obvious, easy latch. Even if he could get them out of this tent, what then? He didn't know the way to the Fair from here. He and the dogs would be lost once they left the circus, and they certainly couldn't return the way Cecil had come. He would have to return later, talk to the pups, and make a plan.

Cecil slinked away, his belly twisting with worry. What kind of plan could he possibly make? He was lost in this strange city, separated from his brother, talking to monkeys and trying to rescue dogs. How had it come to this? The only thing he *knew* how to do was to retrace his steps to the lake and wait for the ferry, which Kitty said might take him to the right train toward home. But he could not go without Anton.

He slipped across the field, avoiding the hustling humans, lost in his thoughts. Ducking under the line of train carriages, Cecil realized that the tigress cage sat silent and very close by. He trotted quickly across the grass. As he passed, Tasha stepped to the bars.

"You're a cat," she said quietly.

Cecil stopped in his tracks. Her low voice rumbled through Cecil's bones. It was commanding. Worldly. She had not asked a question, but he answered anyway. "Yes. I'm a cat." He glanced at her, against Sergio's advice. A bright moon rose behind the tigress and Cecil could see her hulking silhouette, her long tail gracefully snaking side to side.

"So you would understand," Tasha continued. "Come closer, little cat." Her eyes gleamed in the glow from the big tent, two yellow jewels set in the black shadows, and they were fixed on Cecil.

Cecil's paws moved on their own, veering toward the cage as if pulled by a powerful force. "My

name is Cecil," he said, "and I would understand what?" he asked. *Not too close!* he told himself.

Tasha gazed down at him from between the bars but didn't answer. "Why did you go to the small tents?" she asked, tipping her great head in that direction.

Her voice was like tall grass blowing in a warm wind. She was regal and mysterious. Cecil would, he realized, tell her anything. "I was . . ." he stammered. "I'm trying to rescue the puppies. They were stolen from their families."

"Stolen?" Tasha's bright eyes swept the circus grounds. "I suppose most of us were, one way or another. Though many are glad, I admit. But you choose to help the dogs in particular. Why?"

Cecil hesitated. "It's a long story. I'm helping a friend solve a crime."

Tasha turned and sat on her haunches, her chin held high. "You are noble to try, but humans cause too many problems for us to solve." She sighed, a sound like a brook running in the springtime. "Even so, I wish I could at least rescue myself."

Cecil drew still closer to the carriage, gaining courage. "You do?" He thought again briefly of Sergio's warning and realized he was within swiping distance if the tigress wanted to slash through the bars, but Tasha seemed more lonely than dangerous.

"All cats are wild, as you must know." She caught Cecil's eye and lowered her voice. "I need to be out of this place. Free, like you."

Cecil gulped. How could he possess anything that this majestic tigress wished for? "Where would you go?" he asked.

"The forest," she answered quickly, turning away to gaze through the other side of her barred carriage, where a wide swath of dense trees, stretching to the horizon along the water's edge, was darkly visible in the moonlight. "There was a bear here a few months ago, a grizzly. His name was Oscar, the biggest bear I've ever met. He came from a deep woods, and he said if I could get to the lake and follow it north it would take about two days to get up there. It's vast, he said. No humans go there, and it's full of squirrels and rabbits and deer. Running streams, and birds everywhere. Cold and snowy, like my homeland. It's paradise."

"But surely the humans would try to find you," Cecil pointed out.

Tasha tossed her majestic head. "I could smell

them long before they would ever see me. Oscar thought I could make it up there, and I'm sure I could. And once there . . ." She turned back to Cecil and her eyes glowed like suns. ". . . I could disappear," she whispered.

Cecil looked at the tigress and his heart beat madly in his chest. *So far, I haven't saved the puppies, and I'm barely taking care of myself. Can I help a gigantic tiger gain her freedom? No chance.* But he nodded to Tasha. He knew exactly how she felt. "Do you get out of this cage very often?" he asked, peering up at the rusty iron bars, the chains and the latches.

"Only when I do my act in the big tent," she replied. "I go in there each day just before the sun sets. They call it the 'mane ivent,' whatever that means."

"The mane ivent," Cecil repeated. "I'll try to watch tomorrow if I can get in." He wondered what Tasha did in her act, what any of them did. "I've only met the monkey so far, and he told me you have a terrible temper," he ventured.

Tasha lay down in her cage, her enormous paws stretched out in front of her. "I have no time for Sergio's monkey business. He is bossy, a busybody.

Sometimes I think he is more human than monkey. He is afraid of me. Everyone is."

"I'm not," Cecil blurted, wondering if he was foolish not to be. "Maybe Sergio thinks you'll eat him," he said, trying to lighten the mood with a joke.

Tasha purred with what sounded like a low chuckle. "The thought has crossed my mind," she said.

The moon rose into the dark sky as the music and chatter from the tent finally slowed and then stopped. People streamed away, the animals were watered and bedded, and the lanterns were put out. The circus turned quiet, save for the occasional whinny or squawk. And Cecil, alone even among so many creatures, curled up and slept where he felt most safe, in a patch of grass right underneath the cage of the great tigress.

⚜ ⚜ ⚜

The morning brought renewed commotion to the circus grounds as the strangely dressed workers hurried in all directions. Cecil scrounged a meal from the leavings strewn about and talked with a few of the other animals. He particularly noticed the humans who stood waiting outside the gate.

Cecil was just as determined as they were to get inside the big tent. In the late morning he discovered a gap between two of the big tent stakes that was deep enough for him to squeeze underneath, and he found himself in a different world.

It was a giant, round room with a peaked ceiling so high he could barely see to the top. Dusty light filtered down from a circle of window-like openings in the canvas walls. Humans filled the stands and milled around on the ground, their shoes crunching across sawdust and stale peanut shells. Cecil flattened his ears at the thunderous noise of the boisterous people, the blaring music, and a shouting man with a tall black hat who stood in the middle of a large ring, waving his arms. Peering down the aisle, Cecil gaped at four white horses, all with sparkly feathers wrapped around their foreheads, rearing up on their hind legs, prancing and pawing the air together.

As Cecil crept around the perimeter of the room, a slender, quick-moving figure whizzed by.

"Sergio!" Cecil called after the monkey.

Sergio turned and smiled, revealing a row of straight white teeth. "Cecil, my friend! So glad to see you again. What do you think?" He swung his long arm around at the chaotic scene. "Isn't it fantastic?"

But Cecil was still staring at the monkey. "You're wearing *clothes*?" he cried in amazement. Sergio had on a little red jacket, streaked with dirt, and a matching hat that looked like a human drinking cup turned upside down, held on his head by a string under his chin.

Sergio smoothed the front of his jacket with his paw-hands. "Of course I am! It is part of my job. I work with the ringmaster"—he gestured toward the man in the ring—"and together we entertain the people." A bell rang in a far corner of the tent, and Sergio jumped. "Ah, I must go. The cockatoo is ill today, and I'm to fetch fresh seeds for her. Enjoy the show, Cecil!" And he vanished into the throng.

At that moment Cecil heard a familiar voice behind him and turned to see Aclown, the crazily dressed lady from the ferry landing, laughing with a small group of children. Cecil was astounded to watch a clutch of flowers pop into her hand, seemingly from nowhere. Aclown sent the children off and waved to an approaching human who held the bridles of two of the white horses. Turning to the tent wall, Aclown grasped a metal hook and pulled it out of a loop set in the wall. She stepped aside, pulling the tent fabric with her, and a doorway opened up for the human and horses to walk through. When they'd gone, Aclown pulled the fabric door closed and reset the hook into the loop.

While Aclown moved away into the crowd, Cecil sat staring at the latch in the wall. *So it's another way in,* he thought. *Or out.* He crept under the stands and watched a different act, this one featuring a woman riding a cantering pony while standing upright on its back. The woman performed jumping flips in the air, managing to land on the pony each time. The way she rode reminded Cecil of what Anton had told him about the Menagerie. And that got him thinking about distractions.

Cecil carefully observed every part of the performance stage—the curtain hanging behind, the poles, ladders and ropes strung above, the low barrier forming a huge ring around the outside—and gradually the beginnings of a plan came together in his mind. A daring plan. An outrageous plan.

❧　❧　❧

In the afternoon he found Sergio again, and asked for his help. It was a big request, but Sergio was the only creature with the paws to make it work.

Sergio was aghast. "Do not ask me to do such a thing. Think of what it would mean for the circus."

But Cecil pressed him. "Think of what it would mean for Tasha. Not everyone is like you, Sergio. Some of us want a different life. This place is not good for her."

Sergio gazed at Cecil for a moment, considering. "Perhaps it is not good for many of us, hmm? The keepers are not always careful. I remember, not long ago, they fed twigs to the white rhino, but she could not chew them up. And the tigress got bananas! She did not care for those at all, though *I* would have loved to have them." He held his head with his paw-hands, shaking it sadly. "Still, I don't know, my friend. I will have to think on it." And he slipped away, his red hat bobbing as he went.

❖ ❖ ❖

Later in the day, Cecil spoke quietly with Tasha about her act, and he explained his plan. She bowed her head for a moment, then looked at him, her eyes flashing.

"You are one clever cat," she said. "I had almost forgotten what it meant to be clever. But I wonder if we can trust Sergio. He is dedicated to the circus."

"I'm not sure either," Cecil replied. "But he's all we've got."

Tasha shook her head, chuckling a little. "My life, in the hands of a monkey. How strange."

Cecil smiled but said nothing. His plan was full of holes, dependent on uncertain events and unreliable characters. For it to work, everything would have to go exactly right. Other than that, Cecil thought, it was just about purr-fect.

CHAPTER 11

The Rat Pack

I t was maddening. Mr. Morgan required Ruby's help at the balloon field all morning as the detectives searched again, spoke with the suspects, and gathered clues. Anton could hardly stand the waiting, but he needed Ruby's nose as well, so he paced and watched the work. Finally, when the sun was high in the sky, Ruby was released from her duties and she hurried over to Anton, ears flapping.

"I do apologize!" she said. "I thought they would never be done."

"Why doesn't Mr. Morgan have you track the cart himself?" asked Anton.

"He doesn't seem to understand that the dogs are being taken by air," Ruby replied, shaking her head. "He still thinks they are to be found around here somewhere, I believe."

Anton frowned. *They certainly aren't around here anymore,* he thought, trying to focus on the clue at hand: the mysterious "circus."

Anton nabbed a fresh fish from the boy by the lagoon as the duo made their way to the main gate, and they proceeded through with nary a look back. Ruby had no trouble following the trail of the horse-cart along the dry roadway. From time to time she was forced to divert around pedestrians as she sniffed out the path, but she was able to keep moving and soon the pair found themselves far from the Fair, at the edge of a metropolis, staring down a long gauntlet of block upon block of busy city streets.

"Let's do stick close together, Anton," said Ruby. "I certainly wouldn't want to be lost in there all alone."

Anton knew she was more worried about *him*

getting lost than herself. "I won't let you out of my sight, Ruby LeNez."

"Fair enough," said Ruby. She took a deep breath. "In we go."

❊ ❊ ❊

The heart of the city felt like a forest of buildings. Taller than ships, bunched and leaning together, the many-windowed structures loomed darkly over the road. The sidewalks were jammed with people and the road was packed with horses pulling buggies and carts in all directions. The drivers backed the buggies into the sidewalks to park them, so the horses faced the center of the street, snorting and whinnying to each other, sharing news and gossip.

Anton saw strange vehicles he'd never seen before. Long carriages that resembled train cars rode atop silvery rails embedded in the roadway, but were attached by poles to hanging wires overhead, like dogs on leashes. Horses pulled enclosed buggies that looked like tiny houses with windows, and when the doors opened Anton could see people sitting on plush cushions inside. He also saw a thin, wiry contraption with only two wheels, one in front of the other, and between the wheels a man was seated, pumping his legs around in a circle as the thing rolled him along. In the very next block, he saw the same kind of contraption with two seats and two riders.

Ruby kept her nose close to the ground, her eyes forward, watchful. She sniffed constantly and often abruptly changed direction for a few yards, then doubled back. Her long strides were hard to keep up with—Anton trotted quickly behind her as she zigged and zagged through traffic. They plunged past smelly puddles and mounds of rubbish at the curbs. On all sides, people shouted, horns blared, wheels squeaked, engines rumbled. Parked horses neighed to them as they passed.

"Look at the bloodhound!" snorted one. "Chased by a cat—you don't see that every day."

"If she thinks she can follow a scent through here, then she's worthy of her name," nickered another. "What are you after, dog?"

Ruby slowed for a moment. "Trying to get to the circus, my good mares. Am I headed in the right direction?"

Two of the horses tossed their heads uncertainly, rattling their bridles, but one looked at Ruby and nodded down the street. "That's right, keep going that way, bear left at the water. Careful when you come to the train tracks—it can get a little rough on the other side."

"Many thanks," said Ruby as she sped up again.

"What does she mean, 'rough'?" asked Anton, scampering alongside.

"Don't worry," said Ruby between sniffs. "Nothing we can't handle, I'm sure."

As they moved from block to block, the streets gradually became less crowded and the buildings more run-down. Anton noticed fewer shiny carriages, and some windows in buildings had wood in place of the see-through glass panels. Ruby slowed, swinging her head side-to-side, searching for the scent. At last, she stopped and sat down.

"Are we lost?" asked Anton.

"The trail is faint, but I believe I still have it," Ruby assured him. "There are so many other carts that have passed through here already today. Hundreds."

Anton's heart thudded at the thought of losing the path to Cecil. He looked over his shoulder at the congested roadway behind them, then gazed ahead. "I think the water is straight in front of us. The horse said to bear left at the water, remember?"

"I do remember," said Ruby. "That's what my nose is telling me as well. Let's see where the left turn takes us."

❖ ❖ ❖

Anton and Ruby bore left, as instructed, and faced a drab, wide wasteland. It was a rail yard, but no trains chugged along the lines. Boxcars stood open and empty next to stacks of bins and cracked barrels. Weedy grass grew up through slats between the rails. A lone engine, its wheels and pistons rusted stiff, sat on a side spur, hulking and silent.

"These trains are abandoned," observed Anton in almost a whisper.

"Indeed they are," said Ruby. "The big train station near the Fair runs most of them over there, I believe. This whole yard must have shut down."

"It's . . . creepy." Anton had come to respect the trains at full volume, engines puffing and chugging, whistles screaming, wheels clanking. These hushed machines were like ghosts.

"Agreed," said Ruby, carefully picking her way across broken glass and shards of metal strewn on the tracks, still sniffing here and there. "The trail leads straight through here. But there's another strong odor. It's almost like . . . oh, my."

Anton turned sharply to her, hoping she'd found the scent again. But Ruby was staring straight ahead, to the far side of the tracks. Anton followed her gaze, and took in a sight that made his belly flip over.

Four huge rats, black as coal, stood waiting for them.

Ruby motioned with her head to Anton, who fell into step beside her. The pair strode up to the last set of rails and stopped across from the rat pack.

"Good evening!" said Ruby politely. "So nice to see some friendly faces."

The rats said nothing, their beady black eyes shifting between the cat and dog. Three of them were almost as big as Anton, and the fourth was even larger—a fat, oily rodent with a scar running down one side of his face and what looked like a long tooth clutched in one clawed paw. *A hound's tooth*, Anton thought, his whiskers twitching.

"My name is Ruby LeNez," Ruby continued, "and this is my friend Anton. We are trying to trace a horse-cart back to the circus, and our trail leads directly through here."

The smallest of the rats dropped to all fours

and paced in front of the group, making a *tsk-tsk* sound with his big front teeth that set Anton's fur on end.

"Through here, eh?" said the small rat in a high, nasal voice. "Dat's very unfortunate."

"It is," agreed Ruby, sitting back on her haunches. "Perhaps you gentlemen would be so good as to move aside."

The small rat snickered. "Maybe we will, maybe we won't."

"Hush up, Sonny," said a long, skinny rat, his pointed nose quivering. "*I* do the talking."

"Right, Frankie!" The small rat scooted to one side, cowering. "Whatever you say."

Frankie slinked forward. "What Sonny means is, dis is our territory, see?"

Ruby shook her head. "I don't see that. I see a cart path going across these tracks. A path we need to follow to get where we're going."

Frankie gazed up at Ruby's big jaw and drooping jowls. "Nah. You don't understand. *Nobody* crosses the tracks into our territory unless they pay, see?" He rubbed his front claws together in a rolling motion, around and around. "So what you got?"

"Don't be silly . . . Frankie, is it?" said Ruby. "We're merely walking through, that's all. Now if you'll step aside so that we can be on our way, that would be lovely. We're in quite a hurry, I'm afraid." She stood and took a step forward.

The three smaller rats sat up on their hind-quarters together in front of the fourth, forming a rodent blockade. Anton watched the largest, scar-faced rat, sitting behind the others like a king, and recalled his fight with an awful, crazed rat aboard a ship many moons ago. He smelled the grimy, foul odor on the pelts of these rats, heard the clicks of their claws, saw the malevolent gleam in their eyes, and felt his own legs trembling. But Anton remem-bered something else about that battle long ago: he had won.

"Oooh, they're in a hurry," jeered the third rat. "Ain't dat something, boss?"

"I said *I* do the talking, Sal!" Frankie snapped. Sal nodded meekly. "What do you think, boss?" Frankie asked over his shoulder to the largest rat. "They got no payment."

The king rat said nothing, but lifted the hound's tooth in his paw very slightly in a silent signal. At that, two burly brown rats darted out from an open boxcar and raced toward Ruby and Anton, their eyes murderous, their sharp teeth bared. Anton whirled and popped out his front claws, but the rats leaped past him and toward Ruby. The big dog lowered her head, barking and growling, and the rats squared off on either side of her. Behind them, Anton darted from side to side, but he had no angle in to help her. The rats lunged and slashed with their claws, forcing Ruby backward. They maneuvered the bloodhound around the far side of a boxcar where Anton couldn't see her, and the snarling stopped abruptly.

"Ruby!" Anton shouted.

Ruby's voice rang out from around the corner. "I'm all right, Anton. Just closely guarded, shall we say."

Anton whipped around to face the boss rat, his eyes blazing. "Is this how you greet everyone who comes through?" he growled. "What's the meaning of this?" He took two steps toward the rat pack, hissing. Even as he did, his felt his courage falter—there was no way he could fight four of the beasts.

The king rat licked his paws and smoothed the fur on his pink ears for several moments, gazing steadily at Anton all the while. Finally he drew up his bulk and spoke in a thin, high-pitched voice.

"Calm yourself, please. I will allow Miss LeNez to pass through without further delay." He paused, then pointed with the hound's tooth directly at Anton. "But I require as payment that we keep *you*."

Anton's heart pounded. *Me?* Frankie, Sonny, and Sal began to chortle unpleasantly, rubbing their paws. Anton's fear and anger boiled up in his chest. "What are you talking about?"

"We could use a cat around here," Sal explained, rasping unpleasantly. "Cats can catch birds and fish and stuff like dat. We're sick of the usual trash we eat."

"Yeah," muttered Sonny, shrugging, "even though the boss eats most of it himself, anyway."

"Shut it, Sonny," warned Frankie. "Them's just the rules and you know it."

The king rat fixed Anton with a glittering stare. "That's my offer," he said calmly. "The dog goes, you stay."

Anton paused, thinking fast, then nodded. "All right. Let her go." He had an idea—a long shot but one that might free him and Ruby both.

"Anton?" Ruby called, worry in her voice.

"It's okay, Ruby. Go on ahead."

The king rat gave a sharp whistle and the two burly rats appeared from behind the boxcar, nodded to the king, then scampered off into the tangle of train carriages.

"Here's the deal," Anton said to the rats. "I'll stay here while my partner goes on. But I get to choose who gets to eat what I catch."

"You don't get to choose," said the king. "All catches are due to me."

Anton shrugged, looking from Sal to Frankie and back. "I don't see why he gets to say who gets to eat," he observed. "You all share the territory, so you should each get fair shares of the spoils, right?"

Sonny nodded, but Frankie spoke harshly. "Wrong. It's a seniority thing with us. Cats can't understand that."

"But I see what he's sayin'," Sal said. "He's the one that catches, so he gets to choose."

"Nobody but me is choosin' nothing," snarled the king. "And dat's dat."

Frankie turned on Sal and gave him a push. "You hear him. Dat's dat."

"Don't push me, Frankie," growled Sal.

"Hmmm, that doesn't seem fair," observed Anton. "If I can't choose, I think I'll just eat whatever I catch myself."

The rats grumbled. "See dat?" Sal said to Frankie, giving him a shove. "Now none of us get any of the catch."

"Shut it, all of you!" bellowed the king. "I say what goes."

"And I say that stinks!" Sonny shouted, and he leaped onto the king's shoulders and sank his teeth into the bigger rat's neck. Anton took a few steps to one side.

"Me too!" shrieked Sal, tackling Frankie.

The rats toppled into a snarling, gnashing pile, bits of fur and spittle flying. Anton edged past the melee on silent paws and took off running across the tracks. He glanced behind to see if the rats were giving chase, but they hadn't noticed he was gone. He turned and streaked past the rusting train hulks and out along the field where the air was fresh. Ruby emerged as well and greeted him.

"Well done," she said. "How did you manage it?"

"Rats are such rats!" Anton exclaimed.

Ruby laughed. "That does seem to be one thing

we can depend upon." They moved into a trot across the field toward the trees.

The light was almost gone from the evening sky when the two friends began to hear jangly music rising from the white pointed roofline of the circus. Anton gazed up at the spires, which seemed to glow from lantern light inside, and his throat tightened.

Come on, brother, Anton thought. *You've just got to be there.* Because if Cecil wasn't there, he might be anywhere in the world.

CHAPTER 12

On with the Show

Anton and Ruby came out of the woods to find a large field where the grass had been cut low. Across it they could see a long fence with a gate at the center and a banner attached to two tall poles on either side flapping a bit in the stiff breeze. In front of the gate, a line of humans moved slowly past a man who handed them slips of paper. This gained them entry into an enormous white tent that seemed to pour over the grass like a cloud.

"Why do humans line up like that all the time?"

Anton asked Ruby. "They do the same thing to get on trains and boats."

"In general, humans are very orderly," Ruby said. "Even when they just want to have fun. Mr. Morgan likes to play a very elaborate game with several other men, hitting balls around and running from place to place. They're social. Well, we dogs are, too, but we never run in packs as big as the ones humans seem to enjoy."

"So, how do you think we should get into this circus? Stand in line?"

Ruby chuckled. "Now wouldn't that be an amusing sight? A cat and a dog in line for a show!"

"I could squeeze under that tent, but you'd never fit."

"The thing to do is find the horses. They're always near a large entrance."

"And how will we do that?"

Ruby took a long sniff of the air, dropped her big head and took another long snuffle of the grass. She closed her eyes for a moment, sniffed the air again. "This way," she said, and she took off briskly, nose to ground across the field. Anton followed, trotting a bit to keep up with her.

Ruby pressed on, her shoulders and hips pivoting sharply at various points in the track. *That nose,* Anton thought, *that nose. It leads that dog around like a fish on a line. She is hooked.*

That nose led them around the side of the tent, which was, Anton noted, clamped down tight to the grass so that no creature bigger than a rat could get in. Jaunty music issued from inside and human voices rose and fell. There, just as Ruby had predicted, they came upon a large bay horse wearing a halter with a rope attached to a stake in the ground. He was working his way in a wide circle around that stake, stolidly ripping up grass. Ruby barreled up close, nose to the ground, as if she couldn't see what was in front of her. Anton followed, but he was watching the horse, who appeared unconcerned. At last Ruby came to a halt and sat down hard on her haunches, blowing air out of her nostrils.

"Good evening," Ruby said to the horse. "I wonder if you could possibly help us."

The horse lifted his head, and as he did one of his glassy eyes settled on Anton. "An ordinary cat," he observed. "Now you're something we don't see much around here, though there's every other kind of creature in the wide world back there in the tent village."

"My name is Anton," said Anton. "And this is Ruby."

"I'm Henry," said the horse.

"I'm looking for my brother," Anton explained. "Big guy, black fur, white feet, white whiskers. We think he came this way."

"Haven't seen him," said the horse. "But most of the action is either in the tent or behind it." He stretched out his neck, tossing his head to indicate the direction. "They all live back there while they wait to do their shows. It's like a town."

"Do you take part in the shows, Mr. Henry?" Ruby asked politely. Anton knew the great detective was eager to pick up any clues to the whereabouts of the puppies, but she was always careful to solicit information without seeming overanxious to have it. *Set your subjects at ease,* she told Anton. *You'll find out more than you thought you would that way.*

"Not me," Henry said. "The humans spend all their time taking care of the fancier animals, putting on the shows, and moving on to the next place. I do ordinary work, pull carts when they need to bring stuff in, take my master to the town. He's the one running the whole shebang, so he needs a horse he can count on, not some showy, snooty thing that stands on his hind legs and neighs like a fool."

And does your master wear a green cap? Anton thought.

"We've come from the Fair this morning," Ruby said. "We were following a cart that brought a big balloon back from here, though I can't think why they wouldn't just fly back."

"We see those up in the sky every couple of days," Henry said. "Yesterday one of them things went down plop in the lake, or so we heard. Everybody was talkin' about it."

"The balloon fell in the lake?" Anton exclaimed.

Henry nodded. "The horse that pulls the balloon cart, Sedgwick—he's a Thoroughbred, as he never stops telling you—he heard that it was all smashed by the water."

"My brother was in a balloon!" Anton moaned. "He was trapped in a basket."

"I'm sorry to hear that," the horse said. "Maybe he got out okay."

"And," Ruby added quickly, "maybe Anton's

brother was in a different balloon. We think the balloons might be transporting dogs to the circus," Ruby said. "Henry, is there a dog show here?"

"Sure is," replied Henry. "Seems to get bigger all the time. The show I mean, not the dogs. The dogs are little. They keep 'em in the last tent, back there by the big tree."

Anton nodded grimly and took off at a trot in the direction of the tent city.

"Excuse us," Ruby said to the horse, turning to follow her co-detective. "And thanks for your help."

She woofed softly as she caught up to Anton. "Slow down, now. I know you're excited, but it's no time to be rash. We are very near our goal, but these are unscrupulous humans and we don't want to alert them to our presence. I fear we're very clearly not circus material."

Anton slowed, trying to be calm. And hopeful. If only Cecil was in that tent with the puppies. *Knowing my brother, he probably broke them out of there already,* he thought.

"My goodness, what a smell," said Ruby, eyeing an enormous pile of trash at the very back of the field. Sodden hay, paper scraps, and rotting food all lay heaped inside a fenced enclosure. "No wonder I'm having trouble with the finer scents around here."

They rounded the edge of the tent town and came upon a tall spreading tree and a small, mud-spattered tent erected in the shade of its branches. There was a flap open at the front and no guard in sight. Still, Anton and Ruby approached cautiously, coming up along the side, Ruby with her nose to the ground.

"This is the place, all right," she said, stopping on the far side of the tree trunk. "Nothing else smells like puppies. It's the sweetest scent I know."

Anton stopped, craning his neck to see around the tree. "What else are you getting?" he asked the bloodhound.

"There is a human, but just one. Let's have a peek."

Dog and cat rounded the curve and, keeping low, peeked inside the tent. The sun was low and it was gloomy inside, but they could make out two pups being schooled in dancing by a man who pointed at them by turns with a sharp stick.

"Chino," he said, "up. Now you, Bingo." The puppies slumped and whined but eventually stood up on their hind legs. After the man had gotten both to turn around in place, he reached in his coat pocket and doled out some treats. Then he led them behind a curtain and moved toward the doorway.

"Drop back," Ruby said. "He's coming out." Anton and Ruby slipped behind the tree, and a moment later the man appeared at the opening. Without looking back he strode off toward the tent village, tapping his stick across his palm to a tune he whistled in a pitch that hurt Anton's ears.

"Let's make a dash for it," Ruby said, and Anton shot out from the tree. Ruby's lumbering gait brought her up behind Anton inside the tent. Together they approached the curtain, which was open at one side.

And there they were. Six white puppies bunched together, a few asleep, the others lolling about in the straw bedding, in a big wire cage with trays of water and food attached to the side. *Six puppies but no cat,* thought Anton. One of them noticed their visitors and extracted himself from the puppy pile.

"Wow, you are a big dog," he said, pressing his nose against the wire mesh. "Do you live here?"

"No, I don't," said Ruby. "And neither do you. You belong with your family."

Two more puppies joined the first. "We do, we do," they agreed. "But we don't know where they are."

"They're waiting patiently for you to come home and they've sent me and Mr. Anton here to bring you back," Ruby said.

Anton examined the gate, which was attached by a cord between two clamps. "We'll never get this open," he murmured to Ruby.

"We want to go home," the puppies began to cry. "We don't like it here. It's not nice."

Ruby joined Anton at the latch. "If we can't undo these fasteners," she said, "I don't know how we're going to get these pups out of here."

Anton was sniffing the cord. "I think it's just rope," he said. "We need a way to cut it."

"But how?" Ruby said.

Anton grasped the cord in his claws and tore at it, but it was thick and oily, and didn't ravel. He sat back and passed a paw over his mouth. "We need a rodent," he said.

"I beg your pardon?" said Ruby.

"A rodent. A mouse could do this job."

Ruby's eyes widened. "You're right. But where are we to find a mouse?"

Anton looked around the tent as if he might

see one. When he looked back at Ruby she had an amused gleam in her eye. They both said it at once—"The rats!"

"But why would those guys do us a favor?" Anton said.

"You said it yourself—rats are such rats. I think they might if I could lead them to an adequate food supply."

Anton nodded, and again the dog and cat spoke at once—"The trash pile!"

"Let's go and have a word with them at once," Ruby suggested. "We'll be back, young 'uns," she said to the pups as she passed through the curtain. "And you'll soon be back with your folks."

Anton hung back. He knew, had known at once that Cecil wasn't in this tent, but his eyes kept searching in the gathering darkness, longing to find his brother. If his balloon really went down, he had to believe Cecil would have found some way to get out. And if he had, if he'd somehow gotten himself to this circus, he must be here somewhere. Anton followed Ruby out to the sandy grass under the tree.

"I know you're worried about your brother," Ruby said.

"I am," said Anton. "I don't want to leave here until I search for him."

"You have a thorough look round while I go and chat with our friends in the rat pack. I'll meet you here, and with any luck you'll have found your brother and we can gather up these pups and take them back to the Fair."

Anton nodded, his thoughts all focused now on finding Cecil. "I'll meet you here," he agreed.

Ruby turned back toward the front gate. "Good luck," she said as Anton headed in the opposite direction. "And don't forget to use your nose."

❖ ❖ ❖

Anton turned away from the trash pile—it was definitely not the place to use one's nose—and paused in the field to take his bearings. It was evening and the stars were glimmering dimly overhead. The air was still and heavy. Strange sounds filtered through it as mysterious and magical as the flickering fireflies lighting his way. The line of cages was straight ahead, alive with the sounds of animals he couldn't even picture. He heard a high-pitched yowl, a chattering cry, a chuffing sound like a deer but different, a yip and yelp, a breathy whistle repeated at even intervals, an eruption of snorts, and a rasping bark, something like a coyote, but deeper. He couldn't make out what they were saying.

Henry had said the humans spent all their time and energy taking care of the animals, putting on the shows, and moving on. *Why do that?* Anton wondered. It was astounding. Here he was, trying to help one set of humans and a dog find another set of humans who were stealing dogs from other humans and bringing them to the circus in balloons. The real mystery wasn't who stole what animal from whom, but why humans were always moving animals around. Anton's head ached from thinking about it, and he longed to discuss the problem with only one animal in the world—his brother.

He cleared his thoughts and studied the bright scene before him. Where would Cecil go? Would he wander about in the village, where the animals were bedding down for the night, or would he be attracted to the bright lights in the big tent?

Bright lights? Big tent? Anton could hear Cecil's voice, could picture his wild grin at this choice. Of course.

He'd find a way inside, that was for sure. Anton

lit out for the big tent, running full speed. It felt
great to run. Ruby was a fine animal, but she was
an old lady and everything about her was pon-
derous. Anton wasn't going to follow his nose one
more second than he had to. He would use his wits
instead.

When Anton got to the big tent, everything he
needed to distract the guards was right there at
the gate in the form of a small girl throwing a
big tantrum. She threw herself down smack in the
middle of the entry screaming at the top of her
surprisingly strong lungs. All the adults, the ticket
taker, her parents, and two guards were absorbed
in trying to calm her down. Anton slipped noise-
lessly alongside the gate and slunk into the shadows beyond to the wide entrance of the tent. Inside
it was as bright as day, with humans all crammed
into the stands, their heads raised to watch other
humans who appeared to be flying through the air
over a low-sided ring at the center of the tent.

Anton made his way easily under the stands
to the very front. There, he saw that the humans
weren't actually flying, but rather swinging on

various ropes, gracefully passing from one side of the ring to the other, sometimes doing flips in the air or dangling from one foot or hand. They were dressed in odd bright clothes that glittered in the lights playing over them.

But where is my brother? Anton scanned the staged area below. It was scattered with strange-looking equipment. Two men were moving a barrel into place and another rolled a metal pole, with one end stuck in what looked like a tree stump, onto the scene. One stopped and spoke to the other, pointing past the ring to a curtain that hung suspended from a wide bar. Anton had an itchy instinct about that curtain. Something was behind it, something big, something wild. His whiskers trembled with the sensation.

The music, which had been playing cheerfully all the while, began to swell, and the flying humans overhead all lined up on ropes and bars facing the crowds on the stands. As the audience applauded, the aerialists slid down the ropes expertly and, holding one another's hands, bowed and waved. A drum roll sounded as they danced away, disappearing behind the curtain that had attracted Anton's attention. As they went out, a man carrying a stick and wearing a tall hat ran in and began yelling at the audience, who continued to beat their hands together joyfully.

Anton felt all his fur rising, from his head to the tip of his tail. It was the way he felt just before a lightning bolt flashed in the sky. He crouched low in his front-row spot, his eyes riveted on the stage. Two men appeared and carefully pulled the curtain aside. They were quick to get out of the way. In the next moment, the most amazing creature in the world burst into the ring.

Anton let out a squeak of terror. It was a few moments before he realized that the animal leaping about on the stage was actually an enormous black and orange striped cat, as big as a pony. A new man followed her around the ring, snapping a whip this way and that, while the cat, who could certainly flatten the man with one stroke of her paw, cooperated sullenly. *That paw!* Anton thought. *It's the size of my whole body!*

The man bowed to the applause while the massive cat sprang down from the barrel and bounded for the curtain. Anton scooted out a bit from the edge of the stands, craning his neck to see over the low barrier. As he did, the mesmerizing creature turned abruptly, and then something dashed out into the ring, something small and black, with white feet and a white-tipped tail, leaping with wide strides alongside the most fabulous beast who slowed a bit, lowering the great head as if to speak to a friend.

Cecil!

CHAPTER 13

The Great Escape

he atmosphere in the big tent was charged. Cecil's fur stood on end as he crouched in the shadows. Tasha stood motionless nearby, shackled in a metal collar attached to heavy chains clutched tightly by two human handlers on either side of her. They were all hidden behind a thick curtain, waiting for the act before them—four humans swinging from bars and ropes high in the air—to conclude. Cecil could hear Tasha's fast breathing and knew she was nervous, too. He cocked his head up, caught her eye, and sent her a weak smile. She nodded very slightly.

The swinging act ended and the audience clapped and whistled. There was a brief lull, and Cecil peeked under the curtain to see that various lanterns had been set on tall, spindly posts here and there around the space, casting a warm glow over the big center ring. Other workers thumped equipment into place while the musicians played a raucous tune. Tasha's two handlers began speaking to each other, gesturing toward the ring, and the tigress purred softly down to Cecil.

"No matter what happens, I'm grateful for your help," she said.

"It'll work," Cecil assured her. "I know it will." He knew no such thing.

"I hope you find your brother and get back home."

"Me, too." Cecil swallowed, trying not to think of where Anton might be right now. "Good luck!" he said.

Tasha snorted. "Cats make their own luck."

The handlers gave Tasha's collar a shake to quiet her. Cecil saw her eyes go hard for a few seconds and he wondered how angry she might get, if provoked. Then she blinked, and a calm settled over her face. Cecil admired her self-control.

A man with long, flowing hair, dressed in tight clothing trimmed in animal fur, strode up to the curtain. Cecil stared as the man shook out his hair just like the lions in the cages at the Fair had done. Ignoring Tasha and the handlers, he brandished a long black whip in one hand and took a few deep breaths.

Tasha whispered down to Cecil, "That's the tamer." Cecil nodded in understanding. *He* was the one they would need to distract.

In the main ring, the music stopped and the ringmaster shouted to the audience. "And now, ladies and gentlemen, boys and girls, it is time for the Main Event!" The people tittered and settled back into their seats. "May I present to you . . . the crown jewel of Russia . . . her royal highness . . . Queen Czarina, the Siberian Tigress!"

The crowd exploded with applause and everything spun into motion. With a pop of the tamer's long whip, the handlers unclamped the collar from Tasha's neck just as the curtains parted with a sweeping flourish. The music struck up once more, and Tasha and the tamer bounded forward into the ring.

Cecil scooted up to the edge of the curtains

and tucked in to watch. It was an incredible sight. The stands were packed with cheering people, young and old, their faces open and delighted. The golden light from the burning lanterns made Tasha's coat gleam as she stalked around the tamer. To one side stood two ladies dressed in shimmering white, each holding a wooden ring as big as a cart wheel. Tasha had told Cecil what those were for, and he shivered.

The tamer raised his whip sharply and Tasha flinched, diverting around him. He cracked the whip in the air and she jumped effortlessly onto a colorful barrel, one of five arranged in a half circle. She looked at the tamer and waited. Cecil knew she had three tricks to perform. The tamer shouted a command and she did the first one—leaping in precise bounds from barrel to barrel as he pivoted along with her, the tip of his whip inches above her head. The audience thundered their approval.

Next Tasha stood on a larger barrel in the center of the ring, snarling and clawing the air. The tamer approached, pried open her great jaws with his bare hands, and placed his head in her mouth for several seconds. How the audience shrieked at that! But Cecil knew that she allowed it for the act—she helped him, in fact.

"I could give him quite a headache if I chose to," Tasha had confided, and Cecil did not doubt her.

Now Cecil readied his paws for his part in the show. Tasha moved into a trot for the third trick, accompanied at every step by the tamer's whip as she circled the ring.

She called to Cecil as she passed his hiding place. "Ready?"

"I'm ready!" he shouted back, watching as she made one last circuit. As she did, the two ladies set their wooden rings into two tall holders in front of the center barrel. Then each lady touched her ring with a torch handed to her by a clearly terrified Sergio. The rings burst into flame! The crowd gasped and shrank back and the ladies moved to stand by the curtain. Now the blazing rings burned brightly one in front of the other, forming a tunnel of fire.

The tamer grazed Tasha's back with the whip and she snarled at him as she ran, shaking her great head. She slowed as she reached Cecil, sending him a quick nod. Before the tamer could react,

Cecil darted out and fell into step with the tigress, running alongside for a few steps.

"And up you go," murmured Tasha.

In a quick bounding motion he was up on her back, steadying himself and hanging on to her silky fur. The audience laughed and pointed. The tamer's mouth fell open for a moment, but he recovered and smiled as if Cecil was part of the act.

"Well done!" Tasha called back to him as she loped evenly.

"Actually I've done this before," he cried breathlessly. "I once rode a stampeding bison!"

"Impressive." She began to speed up. "Ready for the exciting part?"

"You bet I am." Cecil felt light-headed and he laughed. "Don't miss!"

"I won't! Just hang on. Here we go!"

The tamer cracked his whip twice over Tasha's backside, very near to Cecil's fluttering tail. Cecil yipped in protest, and the tigress cantered straight down the center of the ring, headed for the tallest barrel. Cecil looked up and saw the rings of fire in the air beyond the barrel, and he dug his puny cat claws into the folds of Tasha's coat, pressing himself as flat as he could. Her fur smelled exotic, like wild rivers and jungle trees; Cecil was giddy.

The audience rose to their feet, and the music swelled, filling Cecil's ears. He felt the strength and grace of the great tigress as she ran. In one fluid movement, Tasha gathered herself and vaulted up to the barrel top. Cecil exhaled in a rush, then suppressed a gasp as she coiled again and sprang off of her powerful back legs into a long, soaring glide, an orange and black arrow through the heart of the rings of fire.

The crowd went wild.

"Whoo-hoo!" Cecil shouted. He had felt the heat of the flames as they passed. He had narrowly kept himself from falling on Tasha's bouncy landing, but now he balanced easily as she cantered around the ring. As he raised his head in triumph, he saw a face in the front row of the stands, at once strange in this place but also as familiar as his own heart.

He saw his brother Anton.

My brother! Anton's mouth was hanging open, his green eyes wide with surprise and worry. Cecil's heart flooded with relief, but he had to stay focused on his plan with Tasha or all would be lost.

"Get ready to jump!" Tasha called, still at a canter. She swerved at the edge of the ring and headed briskly toward a long rope hanging from a ladder.

The end of the rope was high off the ground, as high as a person could reach. As the tigress drew near the ladder, Cecil pulled his legs under him and tensed to spring.

"I'm set!" Cecil shouted. It was all in the timing.

Tasha slowed to a trot under the dangling rope and Cecil sprang with all his might. He unsheathed his claws and dug all four sets into the rope, his muscles taut. Success! He was aboard, clinging to the rope and spinning, swinging like a pendulum, just as they'd hoped. Cecil was trying to be as big a distraction as possible.

The audience howled at the sight, and the tamer stood scowling, his whip momentarily still. All eyes were on the swinging cat. But Cecil watched Tasha as she continued her circuit around the ring. Here was her chance—now she just had to make a break for it.

Tasha had reached the far side of the enclosure when the tamer suddenly whirled. His long black whip sliced the air, cracking a hairsbreadth in front of her nose. Tasha reared up, yowling, her huge paws batting the air, then dropped to all fours and twisted away. The tamer darted to the edge of the ring and put himself between it and

Tasha, still flexing the whip. Tasha paced narrowly in front of him, glaring with rage, but Cecil could see she was blocked. Now what? They needed *more* of a distraction, something else to divert attention for just a few seconds.

Cecil glanced around wildly and saw only one possibility. On the next upswing of his rope, he let go, flying through the air with his legs held out wide, and landed on the tamer's hairy head. The audience shouted with laughter as Cecil hung on with all his might, his front legs wrapped across the man's face. The tamer, temporarily blind, stumbled in a circle, trying to pull Cecil off.

In a panic, Cecil looked into the crowd and found Anton. His brother leaped to the top of the enclosure wall in a quick movement. Bellowing, the tamer pried Cecil's paws away and flung the black cat to the ground. Cecil looked again and saw Anton set his jaw and coil to spring, his tail held high.

"I'm coming, Cecil!" cried Anton. In a streak of gray, he bounded into the ring and flew toward the tamer. Cecil felt a flare of pride for his brother.

The audience saw what was happening and hooted with delight. "Another cat!" they screeched.

Anton scrambled past the barrels but lost his footing on the dusty floor. He slid toward the center of the stage and caromed off of the stand that held the rings of fire. Tumbling head over tail into the outer railing, Anton turned quickly to catch Cecil's eye.

But Cecil was watching the stand. It teetered and then crashed on top of the center barrel, sending the flaming rings rolling across the stage straight into the hanging curtains, which ignited like dry paper. The crowd jumped to their feet, screaming. The tamer stared, transfixed for a moment by the flames.

"Now!" Cecil shouted to Tasha. "Run!"

The big cat hurdled the low barrier and galloped down the aisle as if her own tail were on fire. Cecil rushed over, straining to see through the chaos of the crowd. As the immense tigress swept by, men shrieked and held up their arms. Ladies fainted beside them. A path opened for Tasha as the people fled and she plowed on, straight to the tent wall.

Anton rushed up beside Cecil, out of breath. "What in the world is happening?" he cried.

Cecil stood on his hind legs with his front paws

against the barrier and peered after his friend. "Right now, Anton, we need a monkey to have the heart of a tiger!"

Anton squinted sidelong at Cecil. "I'm just going to trust you on that."

Tasha pulled up short next to Sergio, who was hopping from foot to foot, chattering and waving his skinny arms.

"Come on, Sergio!" shouted Cecil at the top of his lungs. "Stop wasting time! You can do this!"

Three figures raced from the ring down the aisle, chasing after the tigress. The tamer cracked his whip overhead, and the two handlers' chains clanked in their arms as they ran. They closed in on the great cat.

Tasha turned to see the oncoming men. She spun back to the monkey, took a step forward, and gave a thunderous roar that shook the stands, echoing across the big tent. The arena went suddenly silent, as if holding its breath. Even the tamer flinched and slowed. In the quiet, the monkey could be heard squeaking pitifully. Finally, Cecil saw a long-fingered paw-hand reach up and yank the hook from the loop in the tent wall, drag back the canvas, and disappear.

Tasha was gone in an instant, an orange-gray blur against the dusky evening sky. Cecil watched the opening for a few more seconds, making sure she had really and truly escaped, then he sat back and exhaled. She had made it. She was free.

Mayhem swirled around Anton and Cecil. Some of the humans rushed back and forth carrying pails of water to the fire while others shouted and waved their arms. The workers hurried to cart away the equipment in the ring, and the audience rushed madly for the exits. Just as the smoke began to thicken the air, the two cats hopped the barrier and trotted toward the open tent-flap doorway.

As they went, Cecil bumped Anton's shoulder and smiled. "Brother, when you want to create a distraction, you really go all out!"

CHAPTER 14

Release the Hounds

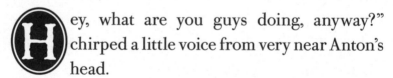ey, what are you guys doing, anyway?" chirped a little voice from very near Anton's head.

Anton opened his eyes and looked at Jasper, Camille's son, through the mesh of the puppy cage. Jasper's pink tongue hung over his chin as he panted in the small, airless tent. Anton didn't immediately answer, and Jasper shifted his attention to Cecil.

"Hey, wake up!" he yipped at Cecil's backside. "Why are you cats in here, huh?"

"Yeah," barked the other puppies, joining Jasper

at the mesh and jostling one another. "What's going to happen? Where's that really *big* dog, huh? Where is *she*?"

"All right, now," said Anton, getting stiffly to his feet. "Calm down. Ruby will be back soon. You just have to be patient."

Cecil rolled over and eyed his brother skeptically. "You don't know where Ruby is, do you?" he said quietly.

Anton shook his head. "I can't believe she's not back by now," he whispered, then turned to the puppies. "Cecil and I will go check what's happening outside, okay? Be right back."

Outside, the tent city was eerily still. A few workers stalked through with their heads down, and the circus animals paced, ill at ease, in their cages on the train track. No visitors waited beyond the gate to see the show; no music played from anywhere. A wide black stripe stained the white canvas on one side of the big tent where smoke from the fire had bled through, and the ladders and ropes of the swinging troupe lay abandoned in the wet grass.

Last night, Anton and Cecil had crept into the darkened puppy tent to escape the humans running in all directions in panicked chaos. Now, the scene outside was like a field deserted after a battle.

"Gosh," said Cecil, gazing around. "Where is everybody?"

"They have all gone to search for the tigress," said a glum voice behind them. Both cats whirled to find Sergio, jacketless, his red hat strung crookedly on his round head. "But they will not find her," said the monkey with a little half-smile. "She is long gone from this place."

Anton stared at the slender creature, who stood on two legs and gestured with what looked remarkably like human hands.

"I'm grateful, Sergio," said Cecil, stepping forward. "She wouldn't have made it without you."

"That I know," said Sergio with a wave of his paw-hand. "And it felt good to help her, I can tell you that." He paused, his round black eyes gazing meaningfully at the cats. "I saw her face as she went. She was—oh!—so very happy." He sighed. "But now I am without a job."

"You can't work here anymore?" asked Cecil.

"The ringmaster saw what I did for Tasha. He is furious with me. I suppose humans will not trust an animal who can do the things they can do."

Anton could see the point. With paws like that, Sergio could steal keys, unlock cages, get into all kinds of mischief. A thought occurred to him.

"Why don't you come with us?" he suggested to the monkey. "We're going to the Fair and it's much bigger than the circus. There's bound to be work for you there. Maybe you could perform in your own show."

"My own show? I have long dreamed of such a thing." Sergio looked off into the distance as if considering, then broke into a toothy grin. "Why not?" he cried, ripping off the tattered red hat and tossing it away. "When will you go there?"

"Right after we get the puppies," said Cecil.

"Oh, *please!*" Sergio gripped his head as if it pained him. "You are freeing the *puppies,* too?"

"We most certainly are," said a smooth, low voice behind them. It was Ruby, rushing up with dirt-covered paws and looking like she hadn't slept a wink. "Hello, boys," she said to the cats, eyeing the monkey as she swept toward the puppy tent flap. "Introductions will have to wait, we've got a job to do."

"Who is *we*?" said Sergio.

"Step back," Anton advised.

In Ruby's wake trailed four enormous black rats, shoving each other and snarling. They ignored everyone, bickering among themselves about dividing shares and who had first dibs. Cecil hissed and Sergio recoiled, but Anton stood with his chin jutted out, trying to show no fear. The rat pack plunged into the puppy tent after Ruby, and high-pitched yips filled the air.

"That doesn't sound good!" exclaimed Sergio.

"Those are the stolen puppies I told you about," Cecil explained to Sergio. "The rats are chewing through the latch cord so we can return them to their families at the Fair."

"Ah," said Sergio. "Well, that is all good but we must leave soon or the humans will interfere. They do not like to lose control of their possessions, even if they are not theirs to begin with."

There was a rustle in the grass and one of the ladies from the tiger act emerged from between two tents. She stopped in her tracks and stared at the trio curiously. Sergio put on a wide grin and murmured to the others.

"Back up nice and slow, as I am doing," he said. "We will make a break for it."

At that moment the tent flap burst open and the

rats charged out, carping and clawing. The lady screamed.

"We did our job, now which way?" the rats demanded. "Which way?" The lean one named Frankie recognized Anton and gnashed his teeth. Cecil unsheathed his claws and tensed to spring, but Anton held him up.

"I've got this, brother," said Anton. "That way!" he shouted to the rats, pointing with a paw straight toward the enormous pile of trash in the corner of the field. The rats slithered off, leaving only their putrid stench behind.

The lady caught her breath and pointed at Anton and Cecil. "You two!" she shrieked. "You were in the show, weren't you? Where is Czarina? Tell me!"

"Does she think we can understand her?" asked Cecil.

"We *really* should be taking our leave now," Sergio muttered.

Ruby bounded out of the tent, six yapping puppies at her heels. "All right, everyone! Let's get this show on the road! This way." She took off toward the front entrance at a fast trot, the pups trailing after her. Anton, Cecil, and Sergio quickly fell in behind them.

"Wait, where are you going?" wailed the lady. "You can't just take the dogs!" She became more shrill, and then her voice was joined by the shouts of other humans.

"Quickly!" said Ruby. "Through here." The circus entrance wasn't manned and the group sped between the gateposts and left the grassy field behind. They circled a large tree and spilled into the abandoned rail yard where Anton and Ruby had first met the rats.

"Whoo-eee, that was exciting!" said Jasper.

"That is one word for it," agreed Sergio, gazing nervously around at the hulking, rusted machines on the old tracks. "And how far must we travel to arrive at this 'Fair'?" he asked.

"It's a long walk from here, I'll admit," Ruby replied. "So let's hold up here for a moment and discuss our arrangements, shall we?"

The animals huddled next to the immense wheels of a silent steam engine and quickly mapped out their plan. Ruby would lead with her nose, a puppy on either side of her. The two cats would each walk between two of the other pups, and Sergio would bring up the rear and watch for hazards along the way.

They struck off in their formation into the heart of the city, the streets as bustling as they had been the day before. Cecil finally introduced Ruby and Anton to Sergio properly and told the tale of the balloon crash and his escape plan for Tasha. Ruby, for her part, explained that when she returned to the tracks the night before, the rats had disappeared. She'd waited them out, surprising them with her offer. The puppies listened to the stories, doing their best to keep up. Avoiding cart wheels, mud, and humans, the squad of creatures was almost within sight of the main gate of the Fair when the puppies began to tire.

"My paws hurt!" said one.

"I have a tummy ache," said another.

"I can't make it one more step," said the smallest pup, dragging his tail along the ground.

Ruby stopped on a corner under an awning, panting. "Look up there, all of you. Do you see that gigantic wheel, going round and round? That's the Fair! We're almost there."

"Don't care about the wheel," said Jasper, beginning to tear up. "I'm thirsty."

Sergio hopped from paw to paw on the hot pavement. "I think we may have a further problem," he said quietly. He tipped his head toward the street behind them, and the cats turned as well.

Anton gasped. The ringmaster stood in the driver's seat of a horse-drawn cart, his narrowed eyes darting from side to side. The cart was headed straight for the group.

"He's from the circus!" Anton told Ruby. "He's looking for the puppies!"

Ruby glanced around. "We have to hide. Hurry, behind here!" She led the others into a shadowed space behind a fruit stand, but Anton stayed on the corner.

"Anton, come on!" called Cecil.

"I know the horse," Anton hissed. "Let me try something."

It was Henry, clopping steadily down the center of the avenue at a measured pace, his bay head bobbing. He spotted Anton and neighed a short greeting, but Anton gestured for him to keep moving.

"Can you do me a big favor and speed up a little, Henry?" Anton called up as the horse and cart passed. Henry looked surprised, but moved into a trot. "Much appreciated!" said Anton. "And if you could take a turn off this road at the end of the block, that would be super!" Sure enough, as the cart reached the next corner Henry bore left without pausing. The ringmaster, no doubt looking only for white-furred animals, hadn't noticed Anton right under his nose. Horse, cart, and driver disappeared down the side street.

"All clear," Anton called, and the rest of the crew emerged from hiding and pressed on, Ruby promising treats to the puppies when they arrived at the Fair.

And what an arrival it was.

❖ ❖ ❖

Anton could see the guards at the gate from several blocks away, the shiny buttons on their uniforms glinting in the sunlight, their flat hats pulled low over their eyes. One by one they turned and craned their necks, pointing to the gang of ten creatures headed for the Fair entrance. Anton knew the troupe must look bedraggled, and that the puppies were hungry, hot, and stumblingly tired. Beyond the gate was the usual profusion of humans, strolling and talking and gawking at the thrilling sights. A large cluster of musicians stood to one side of the wide promenade and blared jaunty tunes out of gleaming golden instruments in time with a snappy beat.

"They call those music players a 'band,'" Ruby informed the others, her tongue hanging out sideways in the heat but jubilant even so. "Sometimes they move about while they make the music. It's entertaining to watch, in a way."

"Yes, I've seen bands before, Ruby, but how are we going to get past those guards?" Anton said. "They'll never let a bunch of animals through." Perhaps they should have tried to sneak in another way.

"Oh, I wouldn't be so sure, Anton," said Ruby, sending him a wink. "All right, everyone, form a line behind me if you would, please." The two pups on either side of her stretched their necks and squinted.

"I reco'nize this place," said one, peering ahead.

"Yeah!" said the other. "I left my mom and dad in there! They're prolly waiting for me."

"Indeed," said Ruby. "Now let's all stay quiet as we pass through the gate. Heads up, proudly now, here we go." The other puppies got in line and pulled themselves up as well, their tails wagging uncertainly, their ears pricked.

The guards at the gate leaned together in discussion, then arranged themselves into two lines, facing inward, with a path through the middle. The first guard in the line winked at Ruby and touched the tips of his fingers to his hat brim. Ruby led the way between the guards as each nodded to her. The last guard gave a signal to the band of musicians, who turned and strode down the promenade ahead of Ruby, their legs all moving the same way, in perfect time with the music. The crowd parted for them and murmured in surprise.

"Ah, wonderful!" said Ruby. "I love a parade."

There was a shout off to one side, and Mr. Morgan burst through the crowd.

"LeNez!" he cried. "I've been looking everywh—" He broke off with his mouth open and his eyes huge, staring at the puppies. "Good heavens, LeNez! You've outdone yourself!"

Morgan disappeared for a moment and returned holding a large, cone-shaped device. He raced to a spot near Ruby and shouted to the crowd through the cone, which made his voice louder. The humans listened, then began to clap and cheer. "Bravo!" they shouted to Ruby and the cats. "Well done! Hooray for the puppy rescue!"

Anton and Cecil glanced at each other and smiled.

"We did it!" said Anton.

"I can't believe it, but we did," agreed Cecil.

Sergio walked on his hind legs, waving to the crowd and bowing. "My friends, I love this place already!"

CHAPTER 15

Moon over Lunenburg

ase solved," Ruby said as the last carriage pulled away from Mr. Morgan's house with the last pup safely restored to his grateful owners. Mr. Morgan himself stood on the lawn having a few final words with the police, who had arrested the culprits as they fled the scene of the circus. The dognappers sat in a wagon, bickering with each other, their wrists clasped in metal rings and the green cap and yellow scarf mysteriously missing.

"These repugnant thieves will be taken away to

jail," Ruby said with satisfaction. "They are doubt-less too old to learn new tricks, as the poor puppies were required to do."

Cecil yawned widely and sank against the side-walk. "Puppies are so tiring," he said. "I still don't get why humans would steal them."

"Those pups are valuable animals," Ruby said. "Quite intelligent, and apparently humans find them to be adorable dancers. The crooked circus owners were desperate enough to try to steal them for their show."

Sergio sat on the step, scratching his chin with his long fingers. "I just hope some human finds me valuable," he said. "I'm going to need a job."

"You'll do fine here," Ruby assured him. "There's no end of work for a clever monkey. I could use your assistance on a regular basis. I of-ten need a hand."

Sergio sniffed. "I get it," he said. "I've seen a world of animals and I'm the only one with a hand."

"Indeed," Ruby continued. "I've reached the conclusion that the four of us make a fine team. My nose is formidable, of course, but there's only so much a nose can do. And I'm given to understand that there is a very interesting case unfolding even as we speak. It involves an empty suitcase that smells strongly of fresh sheep's wool."

"Oh, my whiskers," Anton sighed. "Sheep's wool. What next?"

"That's very curious," Sergio said. "Why would sheep's wool be in a suitcase?"

Ruby nodded sagely. "Exactly."

Cecil yawned again and Anton stretched out, lowering his head to his paws.

"I believe there is a missing jewel as well," Ruby added.

"I love jewels," said Sergio. "I like anything that sparkles."

"Shall we have dinner," Ruby suggested, "and talk it over? I believe Mr. Morgan has prepared something of a feast for us."

Cecil brightened at this news and Anton pulled himself to his paws. The brothers exchanged a long look as they followed the dog and the monkey to the back of the house. Mr. Morgan had put out something for everyone. Fish, meaty bones, even bread, cheese, and a bowl of fruit. Cecil tucked in at once, sampling every bowl, but Anton only nibbled on a fish head. Sergio and Ruby continued to talk about the missing jewel case, and it was clear that the monkey was ready to start work at once.

Cecil wiped some meat juice from his lips and sat down next to his brother. "What are you thinking, little kit?" he asked.

Anton looked up from his meal. His brother hadn't called him *little kit* in a long time. "I'm thinking that it's time to go home."

"I couldn't agree more," said Cecil, to Anton's relief. "And I know the way to get there. From what Kitty told me on the ferry, we're closer than you think."

Anton brightened at this. "Really? How long will it take?"

"Well, first we take the ferry," Cecil said. "That takes a day or so, but one leaves every morning. Then Kitty says there's a train to the sea, and you know when to get off because it's the last stop. From there we'd have to find a ship."

"We might have to consult the mouse network," Anton suggested.

A high voice piped up from behind the step to Morgan's back door. "Did someone call for the mouse network?"

Sergio jumped up from his seat on the steps

and ran to cower behind Ruby. "What was that?" he whispered.

Anton and Cecil exchanged amused glances as two mice stepped out into the open space, their twitching noses engaged at once by the spread of eatables, but their eyes serious in the pursuit of their mission.

"We represent the network, and we can give you very clear instructions for your return trip," said the smaller of the two. "The red train leaves from the big station every evening and arrives at a large city the following morning."

"It's not the red train," his companion corrected. "It's the silver train."

"Is it?" said the smaller mouse. "I'm certain it's the red train. Didn't Clyde say it was the red train?"

"I don't know what Clyde said, but I'm sure it's the silver train."

"Thanks so much for your help," Cecil interrupted. "But we've decided to take the ferry."

The two mice drew their little mouths down into deep frowns. "The ferry?" said the taller one. "Are you sure that's a good idea?"

"What's a ferry?" asked the other.

"It's a boat that goes back and forth across the

lake," Anton said. He turned back to Cecil. "As you were saying, then there's a train, and then one last ship."

"One last ship," said Cecil. He sighed and gazed skyward. "Cats in heaven but I'd like to go sailing into our beautiful bay."

"The kittens will be big by now," Anton mused.

"And old Billy will still be telling everyone what to do."

Sergio listened to the brothers as he finished off a bowl of milk that he held to his mouth with both hands like a human. He set the bowl down and took up a piece of fruit. "You two are home-sick," he said. "I know that feeling. I often think of my mother and the rainforest where I grew up. What larks we had, swinging from tree to tree."

Ruby lifted her head from the bone she was gnawing. "When I was a pup we lived in a small town. I remember the first time my brothers and I had a bath in a big tub in the yard. We splashed like crazy."

Everyone was silent for a moment, thinking of happy times in the past. The mice had listened in awe, and the smaller mouse passed a paw over his nose to wipe away a sympathetic tear. Ruby gazed kindly at Anton and Cecil. At last she said, "I think Sergio and I can handle this jewel in the sheep's wool case."

"So you won't think we're deserting you?" Anton asked.

"Detective work isn't for every animal," Ruby said. "There's a lot of chasing false leads, and in the end someone gets locked up. You two can't abide to see anyone or anything locked up in a cage, that much is clear."

"No," Anton agreed. "We don't like cages."

Sergio let out a hoot of laughter. "I will never forget the look Tasha gave me when I was too scared to open that latch. And that roar! How she tore across the ground to the forest. It shook the earth!"

"She didn't look back," Cecil said.

"No," Sergio said, smiling. "She did not look back."

⚜ ⚜ ⚜

In the morning, Ruby walked with them to the ferry landing. As they arrived, they saw the prow of the little ship plowing toward them through the waves. Kitty, dashing about on the upper deck, spotted them as the engines cut off.

"Hey, Cecil!" she meowed. "Are you coming aboard?"

"We are," Cecil called back. "I found my brother." It was a bright, warm, calm day and it was easy to slip on board past the crowds of humans coming out to see the Fair.

"Farewell friends, and safe travels," Ruby called from the shore. She stood quietly on the dock as the ferry hands threw off the rope and the engine revved. Anton and Cecil looked back, each with one paw raised as the ferry backed away from the landing and out into the lake.

Kitty came bounding down the steps, eager to welcome Cecil. "I knew you'd find your brother," she said, rushing up to Cecil and circling him joyfully.

With her orange coloration and white nose, Cecil thought she looked a bit like a miniature Tasha. "This is Anton," he said. "Anton, this is Kitty."

"Pleased to meet you," said Anton.

"So, where are you headed now?" Kitty said. "Some new excitement?"

"We're going home," Anton said. "And no more stops to see the sights."

"What's so great about home?" Kitty asked.

Anton gave her a puzzled look, then recognized something he liked and chuckled. "You're like Cecil," he said, "always wanting to gad about."

"No more, my lad, no more," said Cecil. "When we get home I'm going to lie about on the dock telling stories to my little brothers and sisters."

"And I'm going to have a good crab dinner and stop by the saloon to hear some fine sea shanties."

"So you just do as you please there," Kitty observed. "I like that idea."

"If we can find our way back," Anton said, "I won't be leaving again. Wish us luck, Miss Kitty."

Kitty sniffed, then gave Cecil a nudge with her shoulder. "Cats make their own luck," she said.

Cecil felt a shiver run right up his spine. It was as if Tasha had breathed over him. He turned to look at Kitty. "Why don't you come with us?" Cecil asked.

❖ ❖ ❖

Two cats got on the ferry, but three got off on the far shore and ran along a narrow road past passengers hauling suitcases and baskets toward the train.

"Follow us," Cecil told Kitty as they trotted alongside the track, staying under the platform the humans were climbing. They passed beyond the passenger carriages to the open cars at the back.

"This one looks good," Anton said, and the three leaped one after the other into the wide, dark interior of the carriage just as the whistle shrieked. The whole train quivered as the engine came to life.

Inside it was cool and spacious with only a few bales of straw and several tall wooden crates. Kitty was quick to have a look between the slats on the crates and announced that they contained the two-wheel pedal carts that humans rode on and sometimes brought onto the ferry.

"Humans," she said, "are just crazy about wheels." With a clank and a groan the great wheels of the train began to turn and the car lurched forward on the track. All three cats rushed to the open door and sat watching the world go by as the train pulled away from the station, heading toward the rising sun.

"This is great," Kitty observed. "You two sure know how to travel."

"Travel is easy enough," said Cecil. "The hard part is winding up where you want to be."

But this time even that was easy. They talked

and dozed until it was dark. Sometime in the night Anton woke with the smell of the sea in his nostrils. He sat up and rubbed his face with his paws.

"Smells like fish," Cecil said, without moving from the hay.

"And crabs," Anton agreed.

Cecil got up from his sleeping spot and stumbled over to the door. Anton followed.

"Do you see where we are?" Anton asked him. Cecil stuck his head out into the night air.

"It definitely looks familiar," Cecil said.

"I'll jolt your memory," Anton said. "Her name is Athena."

"Oh, jumping cats," said Cecil. "You're right."

"Who's Athena?" said Kitty, joining them at the door.

"She's an owl," Anton said.

"A big owl," Cecil added. "And she's nuts. When we get off, go straight under the carriage and head for the front of the train. Stay close and wait for us to decide if it's safe to make a run for it."

"Got it," said Kitty, looking bright and eager. All three leaped from the boxcar and disappeared between the wheels, crouched low and running briskly. When they came to the front of the engine,

Cecil inched his head out carefully, scanning the steel beams stretched across the roof of the station.

"It looks like the coast is clear," he said, dropping back.

"Let's not take any chances," Anton said. "Make a beeline for the street."

"On the count of three," Cecil said. "One, two, three . . ." The three cats leaped from their hideaway and streaked past the crowds of humans pushing their way toward the outside of the station. Anton thought he heard a high-pitched screech as they rounded the corner and burst into the street. When they were well along the second block, Cecil slowed down and they pulled together on the square.

"Where to now?" Kitty asked.

"The wharf is over there," Cecil said, lifting his chin in the direction of the sea.

"Look," Anton said. "You can see the masts over the rooftops."

"Sailing ships," Kitty said. "I've always wanted to go on one of those."

"It helps if you take the right one," Anton said.

They set off across the street and soon came to the wharf, which was well lit with lamps. There were several ships tied up, rocking slowly with the tide, towering over the various men who moved about, talking and working, loading carts and unloading vessels. Anton and Cecil studied each one, looking for some clue as to where they might be bound. Kitty followed quietly, purring a bit, which made Cecil mysteriously calm. The first two ships were huge and deep in the water, their gangplanks nearly level with the dock. One had a horned animal for a figurehead, and the other the head of a large bird. The third was a rough-looking steamer with no figurehead at all.

Cecil stopped at the fourth ship with a sigh of satisfaction. She was a trim, two-masted clipper with the head of a woman carved at the prow. Anton followed Cecil's eyes and sat down with a laugh.

"There she is," he said.

"There who is?" asked Kitty. "What are we looking at?"

"You see that lady?" Cecil said.

"Sure," said Kitty. "She's got long flowing hair."

"Notice anything funny about her?"

Kitty studied the figurehead. "Oh," she said after a moment. "She doesn't have legs; she has a fish tail."

"That's right," said Anton.

"What does that make her?" Kitty asked.

Anton chuckled as Cecil turned to their new friend and said, "That makes her the ship we came in on."

t was the *Sea Song*!" little Sophie shouted happily, as Kitty paused in her storytelling.

Mo, who had been dozing, perked up and said, "The *Sea Song*?"

"That's the ship they first sailed out on, remember?" said Sophie. "They found her again and that's how they got home."

"Right." Kitty nodded. "So those are the three ways to travel in this great world. By sea, by rail, and by balloon."

The kittens yawned and curled up to sleep, and Kitty stirred herself, thinking she'd have a stroll on the waterfront before turning in for the night. She said good night to the kits and set off down the path from the lighthouse to the harbor. She hadn't gone far when she saw Cecil sitting quietly, watching the rising moon.

"Hey, Cecil," she said. "What're you doing?"

"Just enjoying the evening," he replied. "I thought I'd take a walk in town. Anton says there's a good singer at the saloon tonight."

"I'll go with you."

They walked along a little way before Cecil said, "I listened in a bit to your story with the kittens. You tell it well, even though you only came in near the end."

"I've heard your version more than once, you know." Kitty grinned. "There are three ways to travel," she intoned, mimicking Cecil's voice perfectly.

Cecil laughed. "Do I really sound like that? I don't know. Maybe there are more."

"And other places to go," said Kitty, "unthought of by Anton and Cecil."

This made Cecil pull up short. He looked at the moon again, which was bright and full overhead. "I hear the moon is made of green cheese," he said. "Maybe we could go up there and check it out. We'd have to fly."

Kitty nodded. "I've been thinking that instead of catching fish from the top of the water we should find a way to go down to the bottom, since that's obviously where they all live."

"In some kind of underwater boat?" Cecil asked.

"It would have to be sealed up tight."

Cecil laughed. As they turned away from the sea toward the town, Anton met them along the path.

"What a fine night," said Anton as he joined his brother and their friend.

"A fine night to be home," agreed Cecil.

And under the bright moon, the three cats walked toward the town discussing how wide the world was, how varied and fabulous, and how someday they might see more of it.

ACKNOWLEDGMENTS

Once again, our thanks are due to our editor Elise Howard and our agent Molly Friedrich, the first and best fans of Anton and Cecil. We're also grateful to Sarah Alpert and everyone at Algonquin Young Readers for their conscientious shepherding of the cat brothers as they continue their feline adventures.

Kelly Murphy's illustrations have been consistently delightful, inventive, and true to the stories. We very much appreciate her whole-hearted engagement in the cats' point of view.

And finally, we thank the readers of these books, some of whom we've been lucky enough to meet in person at their schools and local bookstores, for their imagination, questions, and boundless enthusiasm for the peregrinations of Anton and Cecil.